BUNDU

ALMA BOOKS LTD
London House
243–253 Lower Mortlake Road
Richmond
Surrey TW9 2LL
United Kingdom
www.almabooks.com

Bundu first published as *Boendoe* in Afrikaans by Tafelberg Publishers in 1999

First published in English by Umuzi, an imprint of Random House Struik (Pty) Ltd, South Africa, in 2011

First published in Great Britain by Alma Books Limited in 2012
This mass-market edition first published by Alma Books Limited in 2013

Copyright © Chris Barnard, 1999, 2011

Translation © Michiel Heyns, 2011

Chris Barnard and Michiel Heyns assert their moral right to be identified as the author and translator respectively of this work in accordance with the Copyright, Designs and Patents Act 1988

Printed in great Britain by CPI Group (UK) Ltd, Croydon CR0 4YY

Typesetting and eBook conversion by Tetragon

ISBN: 978-1-84688-233-3

BUNDU

Chris Barnard

translated from the Afrikaans by
Michiel Heyns

ALMA BOOKS

ONE

It was five o'clock in the afternoon and the yard a sweltering hollow in the forest. I was shaving; the first time in many days. It was painful because the blade was worn and the water lukewarm. There was a glass of wine in front of me on the window sill and after every fifth or sixth razor stroke I would dab more soap on my chin and sip at the wine, and the wine wasn't up to much, but it was wine and it was cold. I made sure, each time, to replace the glass precisely on its little wet ring. And to take my mind off the business of shaving I tried to remember when last I'd seen a human being. Normally Vusi would be somewhere in the vicinity from early to late, but without him the house and the yard and the forest presented a lonesome aspect. Was it de Gaspri, the previous Friday, when he'd brought provisions? Or had Strydom been here after him? Before I could remember, I realized suddenly that the glass of wine had disappeared. I wasn't holding it in my hand; I hadn't placed it in another spot; I'd certainly not been imagining it. The neat little circle of damp was still clearly visible on the window sill. But the glass of wine was gone.

I replaced the razor carefully in the basin and leant out of the window. It must have toppled over and out. But there wasn't a glass on the ground outside. The yard was dead quiet. There wasn't the slightest sign of life anywhere. I looked all around me on the floor.

My almost full not-up-to-much ice-cold wine had disappeared without a trace.

In the previous few days food had disappeared from the house several times. The five strips of half-dry meat from the screen cupboard on the back stoep; the three last stale crusts from the bread tin; a basket of wilted beetroot and carrots from the pantry; the last bottle of preserved peaches that I'd schlepped with me from camp to camp for how many years and had been too stingy to open.

At first I thought it was the baboons. We were in our third successive dry summer and there was no food left in the veld. The baboons came close to the yard every now and again and Vusi had had to chase them from the stoep several times. Even shy forest birds had come into the kitchen looking for crumbs.

The wine gave me pause. Could it really be baboons?

In the kitchen, on my way out to the yard, I suddenly got the sharp smell of sweat. And the screen door was open. The screen door that I always kept latched to keep snakes out was wide open.

But there was nobody in the yard. And there was no sign of my wine glass.

After dinner, when I went looking for my torch in the bedroom, I discovered that both my blankets had disappeared from my bed.

That night I got no sleep. At one o'clock the distant drone of Jock Mills's motorbike was of some consolation to me – a sign of human propinquity. Perhaps because the night was so dead quiet, perhaps because my ears were constantly pricked up, I could hear the Harley Davidson approaching from five minutes away, closer and closer, gradually closer. In my mind's eye I could see the bike making its way through the dark kloof, kilometre by kilometre, its dirty-white beam vibrating through the tunnels of wild orange and brushwood, the dry ridges of grey palm, the long corridors of tambookie, the rising flurries of beetles and mosquitoes constantly vanishing before the beam as if dissolving in the dark. I lay listening to Mills passing by behind the yard and gradually disappearing up the slopes, round the back of Dumisane's hills, and at last fading away over the black crest of the plateau.

At some point after three o'clock, for the first time that I could remember, I went to remove the key from the bakkie and at long last fell asleep with my gun next to me.

I was on the other side of the Bápe near the baboon ravines when Vukile called me the next morning just after sunrise. Reception was poor, but in between the scratching and crackling of the little loudspeaker I could hear that it was Vukile and that he was talking about Vusi. It was a short distance down the valley and across the river to the Mbabala mission station and I got there just after seven. Or almost there. Because Gwaja's procession of skinny goats was making its way to the grazing and it took me a good ten minutes to negotiate the last two hundred metres between the avenue of banana trees up to the whitewashed thatched building that everybody for a thousand square kilometres around liked to refer to as the mission hospital. We generally spoke of the station or the clinic for short.

It had started life as a small Catholic school that on Sundays doubled as a church. In the first few years there had been a dedicated priest, Father Mundt, who during the week taught in the morning and ministered to souls in the afternoon. He started with four pupils and no parishioners. After five years there were more than a hundred pupils, two nuns, an extensive congregation and a clinic on Fridays that was run by Ursula Frisch, a sixty-year-old nurse from Richards Bay with a motorbike and leggings, an unshakeable faith in castor oil and a story that as a young nurse in Kenya she had declined a marriage proposal from Ernest Hemingway. Nobody knew exactly which way the wind was blowing, but there were stories that she sometimes spent the weekend at Mbabala, reputedly mainly because she and Father Mundt were equally besotted with bridge. But three months after her death in a motorcycle accident Father Mundt returned to Germany to be treated for depression. Dr Vukile Khumalo came to start a clinic. But after almost five years there was, with the exception of Father Holm, who had lasted only a few months, nobody who felt up to taking over Father Mundt's congregation.

The little hospital consisted of two eight-bed wards, an operating room, a consulting room, a kitchen, a laundry room, two toilets, two small offices and a long-screened-in stoep. The walls were made of wood and the building was half a metre above ground on stilts.

There were usually a few people under the fever trees outside waiting to be attended to by Vukile or Julia, but even on busy days seldom more than ten. That morning there were probably at least forty. And it looked as if some of them had been waiting for a few days, because here and there under the trees shelters had been devised from sticks and grass.

"Hunger," was Sister Erdmann's explanation when I found her on the stoep, changing a patient's bandages. "Some of them can hardly walk."

"Mozambique?"

"We think so, *ja*. The first day we had thirteen. On Sunday another seven arrived. Yesterday Vukile counted thirty-two. And they keep on coming in."

"Where are you going to find food for them all?"

"Good question!" This was Vukile Khumalo talking from the cramped little office at the end of the passage. Sister Erdmann tried to smile.

"I keep on telling them this is a hospital, not a charity organization." Sister Erdmann would still not relinquish her polite, obstinate smile. "You don't nurse dying people and leave healthy people to starve to death outside." She spoke English with a very pronounced German accent.

A moment later Vukile's heavy figure was in the door, sweating as always, asthmatic, overweight, in his worn white golfing shoes, white shorts, white shirt untucked, battered stethoscope round his neck.

"How are you, brother?"

"Well. What does Vusi say?"

"Much better. He can go home."

"So it wasn't malaria?"

"Dunno. But his temperature is back to normal. He feels much better."

That was always the problem with Vukile: you could never get a real diagnosis out of him. He could sometimes dismiss the strangest symptoms as flu or hypochondria or, if he was really at his wits' end, malaria. Vusi had grown up and grown old here, and the chances that he would contract malaria all of a sudden were exceedingly slim – but Vukile's diagnosis a week previously had been malaria.

"I gave him pills to take. But it's not for malaria. It's for his kidneys. If the pills don't help, it's not his kidneys."

Vusi was waiting by the bakkie, all white teeth and plastic bags of luggage and sugar cane and a grass basket full of young hens.

"Yes, Vusi, how are you feeling?"

"No, I'm good, *mnumzane*. I'm good. Gwaja got me good."

"Gwaja?"

"He says it's my blood. He gave me roots to chew."

"What does he know about things like that?" Gwaja was the hospital cook and gardener.

"Gwaja can see."

"He sees?"

"He sees in your eyes."

I had previously heard Sister Roma saying that Gwaja was an inyanga, a sort of herbal doctor who cured people with roots and bark and herbs from the veld, and apparently also a large dash of intuition. But you hear these things and forget them again. When I asked the old nun about it, she explained that someone like that was trained for years, but that he also relied on guidance from the ancestors.

"Do you believe that the ancestors still talk to us?" I wanted to know from her.

She smiled pityingly. "Of course."

"What does the Church have to say about that?"

"Does it have to have anything to say about it? Do you believe in the saving grace of Jesus?"

"Yes, mamma."

"Can you prove that He forgave all our sins?"

"No."

"You see? We believe in many things we can't see. Those who say seeing is believing, they don't know so well what they're talking about. I see wildfire outside my window every night, but when I get outside, there's nothing."

Gwaja was an inyanga, but nobody ever mentioned this aloud, because that kind of thing would upset Vukile. Vukile refused point-blank to believe anything that he couldn't reason out with his head. He belittled Gwaja's cures and pooh-poohed his successes as coincidence.

Vusi's firm faith that Gwaja could see all kinds of things in your eyes was vindicated. He was covering his hens under a piece of canvas on the back of the bakkie.

"What are you going to do with these things?"

"Don't you eat eggs?"

I didn't fancy chickens on the premises, but I held my peace.

"Julia says she's looking for you."

"Where is she?"

"She's helping the hungry people."

Gwaja and a few helpers had the previous day constructed a cooking shelter of reed and wattle under the largest fever tree behind the clinic, and Julia was in the shelter stirring a huge iron cauldron of soup.

"Morning!"

She gave me just one quick glance. "Yes-yes, the hermit himself! Come and help us stir here."

I was always glad to see her. Her nubility was both the most obvious and the most misleading reason. In the boundless bundu that was my only harbour in a sea of illiteracy and strange languages and superstitions and sorcery and dark unfathomable powers and loneliness, she was the only person to whom I could talk in my own language – in more than just the literal sense of the word. This gave her a head start on the two almost sectarian nuns, the enigmatic Vukile and the tight-lipped, reticent Vusi.

"What exactly is happening here, Julia?"

The spoon that she'd stuffed into my hand was hardly more than a long cleft stick.

"None of these people have eaten in weeks. Some are so weak they can hardly walk."

"Where are they all coming from all of a sudden?"

"They're swarming in over the border. Some down the coast, some into Swaziland, some up at Komatipoort into Mpumalanga. Gwaja says they're Chopis."

"Why all of them so suddenly at the same time?" I knew very well why.

"Gwaja says they were all hoping till now that they'd have a harvest. But this last month's dry heat has made them give up hope."

"Where are you going to find food for them?"

"Stir, Brand."

She scooped a bit of soup into a tin mug and decanted it into a plate and was blowing on the soup to cool it.

"I'm asking. If thirty of them turn up every day, what will you have left after a week?"

"Two strong hands."

"You'll have to decide you can manage only so many people and no more."

She was making her way towards a woman lying in a patch of shade just outside the shelter. There was a baby in the woman's arms, about three months old and reed-thin. The child was dead still and every now and again the woman tried with jerky movements to drive the flies from its face. I stood looking, stirring the pot, at Julia patiently trying to get some soup into the child's mouth with a piece of reed.

"Come and have a look." I didn't realize at first that she was talking to me. "Brand, come and have a look." I could see, when I reached her, that there was something like bewilderment or perhaps even a touch of anger in her eyes. "Who's going to decide how many we can manage? You or I by any chance? Look at this child.

He's…" She shoved the plate of soup into my hands and grabbed the child and pressed it to her. "This child is dying."

The child was lying with his cheek against her shoulder, his naked chest grey with dust, his mouth and nose and eyes caked with sticky green flies, one hand twitching feebly. I went and stood behind Julia and looked at the child's face. There was not much life left in him. But suddenly, in a single flicker of life, he lifted his big head and opened his eyes and gazed straight at me. In all the months after that, through everything that happened, even in the moments of my greatest anger, I could not think away those dark eyes. How long could it have lasted? Perhaps two seconds, maybe five. But all the hungry children of Africa, all the helpless passion and rebellion and anger of all the dying people of the world were captured in those five seconds. The child vomited up the few scraps of soup in his throat – there, take it, it's too late – and closed his eyes. The woman on the ground stretched out her arms to the child as if she wanted him back. But Julia put him down on the ground, because he was dead.

In front of the back door of her *kaya*, later, while she was rinsing her face and arms vigorously under the tap, I was the one who had to brave the sharp edge of her frustration. She wanted me to help her go looking for food.

"Where?"

"I don't know. Somewhere. Babamkhulu's people always have extra mealies."

I had to laugh. And the fact that I laughed was unforgivable to her.

"Who told you that? Nobody stores mealies for longer than one winter. It's just not their way. And after three years of drought…"

"Never mind."

"…nobody around here has enough mealies – not even for the rest of the month."

"I'll manage, thanks."

"I'll take you to see for yourself."

"Without your help, thanks. I'll manage."

"Julia…"

"We need people who can think on their feet, Brand. Not wet dishrags! Go and catch your little frogs, man. Go and count your little crickets." She was drying her hands on her dress. "Go and play with your baboons. Leave us to deal with the harsh truth!"

She went into the house and I was in no mood to go and sweet-talk her.

Vusi was waiting patiently in the bakkie. We were home before nine. The back door was open and the half bag of mealie-meal behind the pantry door was gone.

2

It's always easy being wise after the event. But in fact we should have realized earlier what was coming. The extent would have been open to speculation, but all the signs were there that the Chopis would not be able to solve their problem themselves. Years of civil war beyond the border had gradually made it more and more difficult to sow. Everyone had been forced into a more or less nomadic life and into trying to stay alive like the rebel bands from the scraps you could scavenge or steal from day to day. With the advent of a shaky peace there was hardly anybody left with a fixed abode, a milk cow, a hoe or a little bowl of seed.

Then, in the year of Julia's arrival, the drought arrived as well. That the Chopis had waited until halfway through the third summer of drought before crossing the border was proof of their extraordinary endurance.

We always referred to people "crossing the border", but the exact location of the border was in dispute – as we would discover to our dismay later on. Mbabala was, according to some people, in South Africa, but others believed it to be situated in Mozambique.

If the famine across the border had warned nobody in advance what was to be expected – Julia had. She'd hardly been at the clinic for a week when I went one day looking for relief from a swollen foot on which I could hardly step. Vukile had crossed the river to a patient who was too ill to come to the clinic. "But," Sister Erdmann consoled me, "the new nurse has arrived and she'll help you."

She was a woman in her early thirties with short black hair and dark-brown eyes and an almost too wide, full mouth. Because the nun had introduced us to each other in English, both only by our first names, we spoke English. But only for a sentence or two.

"Is Brunt your first name or your surname?" she enquired.

"Brand. First name. Brand de la Rey."

"Afrikaans?"

"Yes."

"Julia Krige."

"Really? It's almost a year since I last spoke Afrikaans!"

"Brand de la Rey – what a name!"

"Why?"

"Echoes of a rugged Boer past."

"It's been passed down like all the sins of the fathers."

The swollen foot was the consequence, she decided on the spot, of some insect bite. I had to hold the foot in a bowl of near-boiling water.

"It's bloody hot, man – do you want my toes to drop off?"

"You're just being a sissy, General de la Rey. We have to get rid of that poison. The painful part is still to come."

"How so?"

"We'll have to open up the place so that that muck can get out, otherwise you may really lose your toes."

When two nuns and the cook couldn't hold me down firmly enough, Julia strapped me to the bed, plugged her ears and opened up the sore. And not with gentle hands. But I had to admit: the throbbing pain of the previous few days was gone almost immediately.

"You're obviously not as brave as the school books taught us about the General."

"I get my sensitivity to pain from the Brands."

There were signs of infection in the foot and she forced me to spend the night at the clinic.

"What drives someone like you into the bundu?" I demanded when she brought me tea that evening just before lights-out.

"A bad conscience."

My bed was on the side stoep and there was a large storm lantern suspended from a beam in the corner. There was the constant zooming and tick-ticking of huge insects against the gauze and the high-pitched sounds of fruit bats in the banana avenue in front of the door.

"Vukile says you count bugs for a living."

"Something like that."

"Entomologist?"

"My subject is biology, yes. But my interest is ecology."

"I wish somebody would tell me exactly what such people do."

"It's just another form of nursing."

She removed the bandage from my foot and started cleaning the wound. "It's looking better. But I don't like the colour of your leg. I wish Vukile would come back."

"I hope he doesn't come."

"Why?"

"He'll want to operate on me immediately for my appendix or something." She pretended not to hear me at all.

"Why do you have a bad conscience?"

She just looked up quickly, smiled and did not reply. But within the first few months after her arrival on the mission station everybody knew that Julia was driven by a mysterious energy; and they'd seen enough to realize that it could as easily be a bad conscience as a divine calling.

Whichever it was, Vukile and Gwaja and the nuns had come to realize that it was of no use objecting when Julia decided on something. Vukile, who otherwise seemed not really to lament the absence of a priest, confessed to me more than once that he was hoping for a priest to come and rein her in. When the first Chopis started erecting shelters around the clinic and she started dishing out food, they knew that nobody could stop her. Apart from this she had, by way of an exception, the support of both nuns.

I knew that morning, as I drove away from the clinic, that I had no choice – I'd have to go and pick up Julia and take her up river to see with her own eyes that even Babamkhulu had no food to hand out. Because if I didn't take her, she'd go by foot.

I called Vukile by radio early the next morning to say that I was coming to fetch her. Vukile had an odd way of laughing – a sopranoish staccato yelp. Over a radio of which the sound was constantly breaking up, it modulated into the blood-curdling squawk of a night bird.

"Who? Julia?" That cackle made the little loudspeaker vibrate. "Too late, brother. She and Sister Roma left this morning before dawn on donkeys." Again the sound of tiny explosions. "May our dear Lord have mercy on them!"

I left Vusi at home, because he hadn't altogether recovered all his faculties.

In the kitchen next to the stove there was a large tin trunk full of screws and nails and hinges and nuts and bolts and everything that one needs from time to time to keep a home habitable.

"Chuck out all these things on the stoep, Vusi, and see what you can find to keep these doors shut. For the windows we can fix latches, but for the doors we need slip bolts or something so that we can lock them when we're both away."

This was easier said than done, because the house was built of lath-and-clay and poles, and there was hardly a window or a door that was a proper fit in its frame. When one evening during a freak gust of wind I tried to slam shut the bedroom window, the window ended up frame and all in the yard outside. But some scheme we'd have to devise. Gone were the days when we could simply draw shut the back door and drive off.

For the rest of that day I was occupied in taking tallies and checking experiments. To complete the rounds was normally a full day's work – nineteen stations connected to each other by a network of something more than seventy kilometres of twin-track roads on the foothills between the mountain range in the north and the river in the south. For my purposes this was the ideal field of operations because it included marshland, savannah, virgin forest, broken veld, talus slopes and the riverbed.

Most of these stations were unmarked and invisible to a casual passer-by. It was seldom more than a wire trap in a stream, an insect trap in a thicket of candelabra trees, a sough in a growth of reed, a row of vials on a plank in the mouldered heart of a dead jackalberry.

Some stations had, as far as possible, to be visited daily to collect data; others, again, where we had to collect droppings, required only a weekly or some even a monthly visit.

The baboon troop had originally not really been part of my research, simply because quite a bit of research had previously been done on almost every aspect of their feeding habits. But Eugène Marais's more or less scientific writings on his observation of baboons in the Waterberg had fascinated me ever since childhood, even though initially it had been a romantic enchantment rather than a scientific interest. In one of my earliest projects I had tried to get to know more about a member of the gnat family that, so it would seem, bred only in baboon manure. The premise proved wrong and the project was a failure, but the baboon troop in the narrow crevice at the head of the Bápe spruit became my friends and interested me more and more. Due to the nature of their routine I had to be in the kloof either just before daybreak or in the late afternoon when they returned to their sleeping quarters on the narrow rock ledges high above the water. Vusi and I would sometimes make that our last stopping place of the day and till after sunset sit and watch them returning home and uneasily, almost reluctantly, settling into their sleeping places.

That afternoon I was too early. The troop was still grazing on the other side of the Bápe against the low ridges. Under other circumstances I wouldn't have minded waiting for them; it would afford me time to collect data. It was interesting to observe how the drought manifested itself in almost every facet of the system. There were no more seeds and remains of fruit in the droppings of the baboons and monkeys; there were noticeably more excavations under boulders that were too heavy to roll over; all summer long there were far fewer dassies and no fresh droppings at all; because the spruit had dried up long ago, the only birds' nests remaining were those of the larger species like the hammerhead and the eagle.

My mind was not on the Bápe. All day long I had had a vision of Julia Krige struggling through the veld on her grey donkey – she and the ever-deferential, elderly, tubercular Sister Roma; under the venomous sun in an unfamiliar landscape with its dongas and banks of dead redgrass and sickle bush and blackthorn.

I had no idea where I should go and look for her, but I knew that I had to. I didn't want to. I decided time and again that I shouldn't. She would just have to paddle her own canoe. If you were forever bloody-mindedly going against the stream, as she was now literally going against the stream on her skinny donkey, you had to face the consequences.

I walked across the flat slabs of black rock that had once been the bed of the Bápe and climbed up the rock face on the other side. It was not as sheer as the eastern face and so accessible that we sometimes came across klipspringers. For a baboon it was a precarious sleeping place. But at dusk you could look across from the broad ledge and see, right across from you, the baboons sitting on the eastern face waiting for darkness.

I climbed up to a point facing their sleeping quarters. And waited for them. And wondered about Julia.

Where is she? Is it possible to ride in one day from Mbabala to Babamkhulu on a myopic donkey?

The baboons came with the dusk. I sat watching them. The sentinel – the one that we later named Malume – saw me quite soon and kept an eye on me constantly while, taking short breaks all the time, he advanced from ledge to ledge with feigned absent-mindedness. He made no sound in all this time, but somehow the rest of the troop all – one by one – received tidings from above of my arrival.

All of them were watching me.

How the hell did you get your mind around a woman? I'd never known many of them. My mother a little bit. Esta way back a bit. Dear Dirkie slightly. Kristi a little bit more but still only a little bit. Were all of them, deep down somewhere, just like Julia after all, or was Julia different? Was Julia bloody bonkers?

The little that we know.

That phrase often whirled through my head.

The little bit we vaguely surmise. The much that we don't understand at all.

On one occasion my work of months with the amoeba in the culture bottles next to the river disappeared from the table with one swipe of the hand. All because the results had invalidated everything that I had believed up to that point.

The little that we know.

Not only about the amoeba's deviant behaviour; not only about Gwaja's ability to "see"; not only about Julia's strange compulsions – even myself I apparently knew only imperfectly.

Only when the sun had set completely did I spot the sentinel again. He was sitting right across from me, his head half flung back, his eyes penetrating in the last glimmer of daylight. We sat eyeing each other across the abyss, for a whole minute, each with his own questions.

Then suddenly the darkness was there as if it had always been there.

3

Vusi was tinkering with a storm lantern on the back stoep when I arrived home. Where the back door had been that morning there was now a hole in the wall; the door was lying flat on the ground.

"I thought you'd learnt by now, Vusi."

"I was just trying to put in a screw. So I made a hole with a nail. Dwah! There it lies!"

There were no bricks available and he was mixing mud on the stoep's clay floor to plaster the door frame in place, but his mud was too runny.

"Leave it like that. We'll make a plan tomorrow."

"I'll sleep here. I'll guard the door."

"No, that's not necessary. I'm a light sleeper."

The rest of the house was locked and bolted. Every window had a brand-new latch and the front door a home-made slip bolt with provision for a padlock.

Vusi's room opened onto the back stoep. I could hear him dragging his mattress out. I leant out of my bedroom window. "Vusi, do you want to be eaten alive by puff adders?"

"I smeared spit."

"What kind of spit?"

"My spit. Berry spit."

"What kind of berry?"

Vusi didn't reply. He had a way of ignoring you when you enquired after things that were none of your business.

I couldn't get to sleep. The night was stuffy and dead quiet. I lay wondering about the great darkness around me and its mysterious berries, all the secret roots that were dug up every morning before daybreak, all the incantations and pale knucklebones and cobra fangs that I didn't know about and that no one spoke of. Perhaps I with all my little experiments and tallies was unravelling something that they'd forgotten about long ago.

At one stage there were voices in the yard and when I went out onto the back stoep Vusi's mattress was in front of the back door, but his voice was somewhere beyond the diesel tank. I switched on my torch and the argument died down immediately. I could hear Vusi approaching.

"What's the matter?"

"They're looking for food, *mnumzane*. They're cheeky."

At three o'clock I went and sat on the little front stoep waiting for daybreak. There was a pale half-moon in the west and gusts of wind across the yard. No night sounds. Total silence. Usually in summer you always hear bats, bushbabies, crickets, owls, weather muttering in the distance. All that summer the nights were ominously silent.

It had been unfair, I kept thinking, to let her go, knowing that she wouldn't achieve anything anywhere. I should then at least have taken her and shown her. That I had in fact offered and been turned down was no excuse. The sooner someone could persuade her that she'd embarked on a hopeless mission, the better it would be for her and the clinic and the whole area. Because the longer there was a rumour circulating that the mission hospital next to the river had food for hungry people, the more people would stream there, and the less able the station would be to meet the need. Instead of a source of hope it would be transformed overnight into a giant cemetery.

At sunrise I helped Vusi to plaster the back door into the wall.

Two hours later I was on my way.

TWO

I

There was no road to Babamkhulu's kraal. Some of his people sometimes came by foot to ask for help at the hospital, but very rarely. They probably reached the dirt road from the south by cattle trails or otherwise simply kept next to the river through the veld.

To follow a donkey's trail through the veld in a vehicle is well-nigh impossible. You have to stop every hundred metres to look for hoof prints, and more often than not make huge detours where the animals can take short cuts through dongas and dry riverbeds.

I kept as close as possible to the river. And still had to stop every few kilometres to criss-cross the area on foot looking for hoof prints. And found nothing. Twice cattle tracks; a few times reedbuck prints; once a single leopard spoor, about two days old, in a sandy patch between the huge roots of a wild fig.

Babamkhulu's kraal was probably a good sixty kilometres as the crow flies from the mission station. Through the veld in a vehicle, with all the detours you had to take, perhaps seventy or more. All the stopping and searching, the getting stuck in sandbanks and ditches and in unforeseen aardvark burrows delayed me more than I'd anticipated. I'd left the station at ten; at two o'clock that afternoon I could still not see the scattered rocky hillocks behind Babamkhulu's kraal, and those hillocks were visible for a good twenty kilometres from the west.

I stopped under a stretch of hook thorn near the river and walked down to the water. The stream hadn't run for months;

all that remained were stagnant pools among the smooth, black slabs of rock. There were no tracks by the water. I turned round and started making my way back, my eyes on the ground, looking for a sign of human footprints or donkey tracks – past the hook thorns. There was little grass. In places you could walk for twenty paces without stepping on a so much as a tuft. I knew I'd have to carry on walking until I found the tracks. They'd had a start of more than twenty-four hours on me; the chances that I could be ahead of them were exceedingly slim.

After a kilometre I started doubting.

If Julia had been on her own, I would have assumed that she'd gone off course. But Sister Roma was with her, and she had not only grown up here, she regularly worked on foot in the vicinity among the sparsely scattered settlements.

There was only one plausible explanation for why they'd strayed so far from the river – to avoid the trees and shrubs of the low-lying areas and to move into more open veld.

I started moving away from the river towards open territory.

In a bare patch almost entirely without grass and with only little clumps of guarri and sickle bush here and there, almost two kilometres from the river, the tracks were suddenly clearly visible in the sandy red soil before me – the characteristic angular indentation of a donkey trotting.

I went to fetch the bakkie and followed the trail for more than an hour.

Just before five in the afternoon it was at first just a dash of colour under a flatcrown. Fifty metres farther it was Julia and Sister Roma loading the donkeys.

I stopped next to them and got out.

"Brother Brunt! Hello!" The nun with the thousand wrinkles on her cheeks was always glad to see one.

"*Yebo, mama. Kunjani?*" (How are things?)

Julia kept her back turned on me while fiddling with her donkey's saddlebag.

"Afternoon, Julia."

"Afternoon." She was clearly not at all in the mood for my company. Sister Roma could speak no Afrikaans; Julia no Zulu. I decided to speak Zulu.

"How are things, *mama*?"

"We are healthy. But we're struggling. The donkeys are headstrong. There's nothing here for them to eat." Then she switched to English. "Have you come to look for us?"

I stuck to Zulu. "I'm coming to ask you to turn back. You know just as well as I that Babamkhulu has no food to give away. Not even food to sell. Perhaps not even enough food for his own people. But I'll drive there and ask him. And if he has, I'll bring. But turn back."

"Would you mind speaking English?" Julia asked.

Then I switched to Afrikaans. "I'm talking to someone who can see reason. It's clear that you can't."

She decided to ignore me. "Come, Sister. We must try and reach the river before dark."

"Wait. Brother Brunt says—"

"I don't care what he says. We still have a long way to go." Julia got hold of her donkey by its bridle and pulled, quickly, angrily. And the donkey did what headstrong donkeys do and jerked back, yanking the bridle from her hand and moving off to one side. Just as stubborn as she.

"I'll drive and go and look for meal, Julia. But I want you to come along. You have to see with your own eyes."

"And leave Sister Roma here on her own?"

"She can come along."

"And I suppose you load the two donkeys in the back."

"We unsaddle them and give them a slap on the rump. They'll be back at the station before twelve o'clock tonight."

"Are you crazy? These are Gwaja's donkeys. I promised him we'd bring them back safely."

She tried to grab the donkey by the bridle, but he was just too fast for her every time. He'd watch her distrustfully while she approached cautiously, and then jerk his head away just before she could grab the bridle. I could see she was tired and just as fed up with the donkey as with me.

"Wait, I'll get it." Sister Roma was moving around the back of the donkey. She rubbed his neck and took the bridle and handed it to Julia. "Maybe you should go with Mr Brunt; I'll take the donkeys back."

"Never. We can't leave you on your own. Not with two donkeys. Look where the sun is, Brand!"

I was sure that she wouldn't accept the offer; indeed, I was convinced that she would accept absolutely nothing from me. So I said, more from irritation than anything else: "Man, I'll take the bloody donkeys home. You take the bakkie and go and see."

She didn't hesitate for a moment. "Come, Sister." She was on her way to the bakkie already. "Let's go. Brand will take the donkeys back."

2

For a good while after sunset I could still see quite well in the afterglow glimmering out behind the horizon and hovering like phosphorus around the trees. The donkeys knew they were on their way home and they were in just as much of a hurry as me. There was a measly moon at three o'clock and there were no clouds.

The ears of the two beasts were twitching all the time. They were in a hurry but anxious. From time to time they both stopped dead and gazed for a while into the grey darkness, like Strydom when the lamplight catches his cracked spectacle lens at a wrong angle, but then they started walking again.

We trudged on until the moon had almost set. Then I knee-haltered the animals and tied one to the low overhanging branch of a fig tree. Twenty metres away there was a sizeable guarri bush in a patch of grass half in the clearing. I nested down on the sunrise side of the guarri and waited for sleep. It must have been about three o'clock.

I could hear the untied donkey grazing farther and farther away. And far away, bitterly far away, like all that summer long, and the previous summer, as if on a different continent, there was a flickering of lightning from time to time, like the wing of a sparrow stirring in its sleep – so slight that time and again one had to concede that it might just be one's imagination. I lay waiting for the sound of thunder. And knew I was waiting in vain. There was nothing. I lay waiting for any sound. A jackal, a nightjar, plovers, anything. There was nothing. Only the dry leaves rustling from time to time. Later it was easy to imagine I could hear a moth spreading its wings somewhere close to me, next to my cheek; I could hear ants walking; I could hear pupae stirring somewhere deep under the dead soil.

All the time I was trying not to wonder about Julia.

In the beginning, just after I'd got to know her, it wasn't like that at all – but later I told myself more and more that I didn't really like her. She's too strenuous, too headstrong, too confused for my taste. But the more I tried to convince myself of that, the more nights I lay awake over her. That night in the guarri I knew I was addicted to her and scared of her because I knew that she could bugger up my whole life for me.

I relived again and again the moment when Julia suddenly turned to me. There was something in that moment that only she and I knew about. The moment that she knew I capitulated: I'm throwing in the towel: I'll take the donkeys home. "Come sister," I heard her say again and again. "Let's go." Just like that. "Brand will take the donkeys back." Sister Roma had probably expected anything but that. She knew us by now. She knew there'd be a squabble: many words, brooding silences, new eruptions. She hadn't expected this new turn of events. And when it came, she was caught so unawares that she dropped the little cloth bag of stuff that she'd been fiddling with, before she'd tied it up properly. It fell next to her donkey on the bare soil and I was too quick for her – she was still going to bend down, when I was already picking it up. Three crests of a tortoise shell, a little worn wooden cross, three gleaming lala seeds, the prickly tip of a jackal tail, a single knucklebone, four porcupine quills, a little string of prayer beads. "Oh, thank you, Brunt," was all she could say. "Thank you. You are so kind. Thank you!" She held open the cloth while I packed everything away, knotted it closed and pushed it into her apron pocket.

"Thank you, my dear."

I knew, at that moment, that I understood more about her than ever before; almost more than about myself, because I'd seen something of her that I'd not yet discovered about myself.

Now and again I drifted off, legs pulled up to my chest, my hands cupped over my face, and in the vague, fluid landscape just this side of sleep I knew I was smelling Sister Roma's cloth-bag knucklebone and tortoise shell; I smelt donkey; I smelt jackal and lala seed. I could see myself lying in a limitless twilight of unfamiliar things.

Somewhere this side of four o'clock I went looking for the loose donkey and tied it to the fig tree and let the other one graze. And then for the first time slept fast.

Before sunrise I had the donkeys in hand. I slapped the back one on the rump and followed while they trotted ahead farting and frisky.

We got back to the mission station in the early afternoon. Julia and Sister Roma hadn't got back yet.

Vukile, dripping with sweat behind his little home-made desk, was actually too preoccupied with his own problems to pay me any heed – but he just couldn't resist the temptation first to have a good laugh.

"What was that guy's name again? The mad Spaniard with the donkey?"

I was in no mood to refresh his memory.

"How come you end up with the donkeys, brother? Did she knock you over the head and take your keys? Or didn't it require violence?" Vukile had enough problems of his own. The camp behind the clinic had almost doubled in size overnight. The whole of the backyard and the plot of open ground between the yard and the church was now full of little branch shelters and ragged blankets and people talking at the tops of their voices or lying in the sun sleeping or just sitting.

The little courtyard in the hospital where Vukile examined his patients every morning was so full of people that one could hardly move. There were mostly women with children, and because there were so many runny tummies and open sores and so much mucus the whole courtyard was caked with flies.

"I can't keep up." Vukile was seldom anything other than tranquil, but that afternoon there was something panic-stricken in his attitude.

"My medicine is running out. We're not getting any sleep. We've had five deaths so far this week. We'll have to find help."

"I see Gwaja's goats are all rickety with hunger. Why don't you slaughter the beasts?"

"What? We've licked him clean. Julia's even offered to buy goats from him, but he refuses. He says his goats are holy."

"These people can't just move in here. If I were you, I'd send them to Jozini."

"None of these people would make it to Jozini."

"Why don't you phone Ulundi?"

"They're all talk. I phone every day. Long stories. They say they're negotiating with Maputo. What can Maputo do? Maputo is getting depopulated."

He was handing out pills. But as usual it was the nearest pill for the nearest patient. Everyone at the clinic had at some stage wondered aloud whether Vukile had any qualification beyond the BSc certificate on his office wall; but nobody wanted to ask, because just as he was hazy about his past, so was he touchy about anything that could be interpreted as a motion of no confidence. The night when Sister Erdmann's appendix had to be removed, the whole station's inhabitants spontaneously decided to make it a night of earnest prayer. She did turn around at death's door, but that she survived at all was afterwards ascribed by everybody to her exceptionally strong constitution and to the Lord's miraculous grace.

That she afterwards always walked with a slight stoop, probably because her intestines had been sewn together, was accepted as a very modest price to pay.

Julia and Sister Roma had not returned by sunset.

It was dark soon. Vukile and the few helpers were all caring for patients and crying children. I tried to lend a hand, but was more in the way than anything else. "Take the child, brother, and go and sit with him on the stoep. Shake him if he cries. He's hungry, that's all." I remembered the child who had died before my eyes two days previously and hoped it wouldn't happen again, because this child, too, was just skin and bones and very limp and alarmingly still. I went to sit by the storm lantern on the side stoep with the child on my lap. The gauze was caked with praying mantises and outside the trunks of fever trees showed ghostly white in the dancing light of the cooking fire.

Because he was so emaciated, it was difficult to guess the child's age. Perhaps three, perhaps older. The face was old. There were notches around the mouth, and the neck was the neck of a very old, wrinkled person. The eyes were sunken into the head. They were tired, sad eyes. They shone dully and dark brown like Roma's lala pips. And I realized, suddenly, when I twisted my body slightly and the light fell more brightly, that the child was looking me squarely in the eyes, like the previous one that morning in Julia's arms. And there was something in those age-old eyes that reminded me of the distant light in the sentinel's eyes that afternoon in the kloof. An inexplicable, fathomless, painful melancholy at the great and unknown darkness ahead.

3

Sometime after nine the bakkie's lights could be seen approaching through the forest and swerving up into the avenue of bananas. The child was asleep on my lap. I went and pressed him into Sister Erdmann's arms and went out with the storm lantern to where the bakkie was pulling up next to Julia's *kaya*. I could see in passing that there was nothing in the back. Julia hadn't switched off the engine. The window was closed and she was just sitting there gazing ahead of her. Even when Sister Roma got out and came round the front of the bakkie rheumatically, half blinded by the headlights, Julia remained sitting stock still. The nun said nothing – just put her hand on my arm and walked past me to the hospital.

The bakkie was evidently still in gear, and when Julia took her foot off the clutch, the vehicle lurched forward and died. I opened the door and switched off the lights.

"Hello, Julia."

"Hello."

"Travelled well?"

"Thanks." I could see it was an effort for her to get out of the bakkie. She had to hold on to me for a moment to find her feet. "My feet have gone to sleep."

"Try a hot shower. I'll come and say goodbye before I leave."

"The tank is empty. You'll have to pump diesel."

The evening was stuffy, but I could feel the heat radiating from the engine. The poor thing had probably been driven in second and third gear all day. In Julia's bedroom window behind the papayas a feeble light was trying to assert itself in the darkness. I poured some diesel from the spare can, checked the water and oil, and went to say goodbye to Vukile.

"Never! It's half-past nine, brother; you can't go now."

"I've got work to do, Vukile. And I'm tired. Nobody is going to get any sleep around here tonight."

"That's no lie!"

Outside in the yard with the little crescent moon of the previous night riding just above the black ridge of the horizon like a ship adrift on a dark sea, Vukile and I were both a bit awkward for a moment, because suddenly there was nothing for us to say to each other. Vukile must have known of the bakkie's empty back, but he didn't talk about it – and because we both preferred not to mention it, there was nothing else to say. We bade farewell wordlessly and separated, each to confront his own questions.

Julia had had her shower. There was a towel around her neck. Her hair trailed in strings around her head and she was eating a banana.

"Come in."

"I must get going."

"Stay here. Please."

"Julia, I still have to…"

But she dragged me into the room by the hand. "Please."

There were five bunches of half-ripe bananas and a few papayas on the table.

"I think it's Gwaja who comes to hide the stuff here. He complains that the people pick everything while it's still green."

Her house was just three rooms – a sitting room-dining room-kitchen, a bedroom and a shower-toilet. The furniture was homemade. Against the walls and in hand-carved wooden bowls were tree seeds, calabashes, clumps of loerie and guinea-fowl feathers, porcupine quills, strings of beads, everything permeated with the incense that she was so fond of burning.

"Thanks for your bakkie."

"Don't mention it."

"Thank you for bringing back the donkeys. Or didn't you?"

"I did."

"Babamkhulu has nothing."

I broke myself a banana from the bunch and peeled it.

"We went on to Tungu's kraal. He doesn't have anything either."

"Nobody has, Julia."

"Will you stay here tonight?"

"Why?"

"Because I'm damned if I know what to do next, Brand. Because I've… run out of ideas. I…" She took the towel from her shoulders and started drying her hair. And when she spoke again, it was quite calm and sober. "If you feel up to staying, I'd… be pleased. I'll make us something to eat. We needn't talk. You must be just as tired as I am."

"We can eat green bananas."

"I don't feel up to being on my own tonight."

Like the hospital and the church and the nuns' quarters, her house was on stilts – but against an incline: the back was almost level with the ground; the front opened onto a small balcony some two metres above the ground. We went and sat on the balcony listening to the voices behind us under the fever trees and to a single bat somewhere among the bananas.

"I don't understand what's happening here," she said once. "I don't understand why such things happen. But what really just… flabbergasts me, is that you… I'm sorry, fine, I knew I said we needn't talk, but I don't understand how you can just shrug off what's happening here!"

"Can I try answering that?"

She wanted to say something, but she thought better of it and sighed and said: "…Yes."

"You can help twenty people for maybe six months. With food. And medicine. Whatever. And forty people maybe three months. And eighty people maybe six weeks. But because the bush telegraph works as it does, in a week's time you won't have any food for anybody. What then?"

"Good excuse, Brand."

I got up and went into the house. Looked for a candle. I wanted to take a shower.

"Rather just say you don't want anybody here because it buggers up your research."

"That's also true. But it's not the only reason."

"You'll let hundreds of people starve as long as you can carry on with your little experiments. That's the part of you that I…"

I closed the shower door and opened the tap.

From her point of view there was some truth in what she'd said. It wasn't grabbed from thin air. But viewed from the other side, it was totally untrue. If my research was threatened I would move mountains to ward off the threat. Attracting hungry people with food and medicine was the best possible way of ruining my research. But there were assuredly other ways of alleviating the plight of the hungry.

The steaming water on my body was like a miracle happening. I could feel it washing away the tiredness. I soaped my body and felt I was cleaning myself properly for the first time in years.

There were stories in the bush about Jock Mills. Apart from all the many other stories, there was the one that was being told and retold more and more frequently about the plane he was supposed to be building beyond the Dumisane hills; a plane that had come to grief in the bush war and that he was rebuilding piece by piece. Some said it was a Boeing; others maintained it was a two-seater whatever. Probably it was something in between, because the air force had used neither Boeings nor two-seaters. Ten to one it would be a Hercules or a Dakota. And if it was, we might be able to use it to ship off the whole crowd of people somewhere else. Where they could be given proper care.

Except of course that Jock Mills was hardly the person to swing something like that with ease. Somebody else, perhaps. But not he.

When I opened the shower door and the steam started dissipating, I could smell toast, and fried bananas and something like peanut butter. And incense. The table had been set. There was a can of cold beer and a serviette next to my plate. And a side plate with celery and radishes.

"That looks good."

I could not see her, but the *kaya* was so small that people could hear each other everywhere. She was in the bedroom combing her hair.

"Have your beer so long." When she sat down at table a while later she was no longer in her white uniform. "Bon appétit! I realized today that I'm crazy."

"Me too."

34

"You're crazy too?"

"No, you."

"Oh. I was going to say. You're not quite the type to ever realize you're crazy. For that you're too considered."

"The toast is good, Julia."

"Why? What's wrong with the banana?"

"Why are you crazy?"

"Because – I mean, look at me. Here I go buggering through the godforsaken bundu in a borrowed bakkie with an ancient nun right in the middle of a hellish famine praying all the way, searching for a few mealies here and a bag of sweet potatoes there and… Hell, Brand, do you get the picture?"

"More or less."

"I could have been walking next to the Seine or sitting praying in Notre Dame. Or I could have been baking a milk tart in some kitchen in Randburg or been in bed with a lover in the Vineyard in Cape Town. Why the hell am I here at all, Brand?"

"Because you've tried all the other options."

"Except the milk tart."

I could only shrug and hope the topic had been exhausted. But she hadn't finished. "What are *you* doing here?"

"I'm trying to get to understand more about the world."

"Here?"

"Precisely here."

"Yes, I know there's a rock face and a vlei and a river and all. But the whole country is full of such places."

"Oh good grief, Julia! That's exactly my point."

"What?"

"There are very few places in the country where I'll find what I have here without any human factor. It's like Paradise the day before Adam was created. You'd have to go far to find something like it."

"What about us sitting here? Bang in the middle."

"It's fifty kilometres from where I work."

"So? Why do you see these Chopis as a threat?"

"Because they've reached me too. Next thing we see, it's water pollution and snares and veld fires. And gone is seven years' work. Which I'll never be able to replicate elsewhere."

"So what are we to do?"

"We must help the people to reach a place that's equipped to care for them."

"How?"

We carried on eating in silence. If for no other reason than that we were both at last too tired to talk.

4

It was not exactly as if our relationship needed that summer's drama. That's to say if one could even call it a relationship at all. It had actually from the start been a kind of ceasefire that was broken from time to time. I was slightly cracked on her and had said so to her more than once. She, in her turn, was not nearly as outspoken, and yet she showed enough to make me feel that there was also a kind of attraction from her side. But neither of us was ready for a love affair. Both of us were in a certain sense at a stage of our lives where we couldn't afford an emotional commitment. On the other hand Julia, in particular, had been through the mill often enough to know that there was too much at stake for just a fling.

I did from time to time tell myself that she probably found me overly naive about love. Either that, or she was scared that I'd treat her as I'd treated Kristi. After all, her relationships with men had all ended on the same note; every time like the final scene of some melodrama.

In a sense we'd never been closer to each other than in those two or three months after her arrival at Mbabala. It was the summer of the last year of rain. It had rained more than enough. All the spruits and pans and rivers were full. The bush was lush. I went to visit the mission station often and fetched her a few times to spend the weekend with me. Sister Erdmann was not at all happy about this – especially the time the river came down in flood and Julia was trapped on my side of the bank for two days. But Sister Erdmann needn't have worried. We both of us still had too many barricades in place that would have to be dismantled – for the time being we were perfectly happy just to have each other's company. We climbed the ravines around the Bápe and swam in the pools; I helped her in the hospital; we played chess and went for walks in the rain and sat for hours talking on the balcony of her *kaya* by starlight. Because there was so much to talk about; there were two lifetimes of stories to be exchanged. And there was of course the possibility, for both of us, that the other might just, conceivably, become a kind of answer to some unformulated question.

The level-headed side of me was quite convinced that she could never be a permanent part of my life. Her restless spirit would always yearn after something else, something nameless, something beyond the cosy present. Every story she told me confirmed this. Her high-school years as a political activist, her eighteen mixed-up months at university, her reckless year in Europe, her two years in the convent and the travail afterwards, her year with Jan Tolmay in Johannesburg. She was ever and ever again searching for some-thing else. I would probably turn up at Mbabala one day to hear that she'd disappeared – walked off – de Gaspri had picked her up. She's gone. Into thin air.

That evening at the supper table, with nothing left to say to each other, I once again got the feeling I'd had a few times before – that our relationship had come full circle. And I couldn't understand how it had come about that there was nothing inside the circle; in a sense everything between us was over before it had started. To me it seemed familiar – for her it was probably a novelty.

After supper I went to sit in a deckchair on the stoep listening to Julia clearing up and washing the dishes. Later she came out and sat down next to me. "Do you understand," she said after a while, "that I have certain things that I *must* do?"

I knew at once what she was referring to. "Yes."

"But as in *really* must."

"I don't know if I always understand completely, but I know what you're saying, Julia."

"I don't expect anybody else to understand the why, because I don't understand it myself. All I know is that that's the way it is."

"Yes."

"Because I... It'll be dreadful if one day you have to tell me that I misled you or misused you or whatever."

"You've never given me any undertaking."

"Why did you decide to stay here tonight?"

"Because you asked me to."

"Was that reason enough?"

"And because I wanted to."

"I think it's because it's been done to me too often that I never, ever want to do it to somebody else. And especially not to you."

"Are you referring to Tolmay?"

"To Ulrich. Ag, I suppose Jan Tolmay was no more than I deserved. But Ulrich I was really not expecting. I could have married Ulrich. I think."

She met Ulrich Neumann on the first day she arrived in Paris. She was lost and bewildered and with a rucksack on her back and a suitcase in each hand searching for the Rue de Vaugirard somewhere on the Left Bank near the Sorbonne. Ulrich showed her the way, helped her past the rude concierge and carried her luggage for her up the dark staircase to the green garret-room door on the sixth storey. He dragged her along from one bistro to the next, showed her the city, taught her to fish in the Seine and to travel by metro. They picnicked in the misty forests of Fontainebleau and lit a candle in every cathedral in the city. He kissed her one morning at three o'clock on the steps of the Odéon and a month later moved in with her. They hitch-hiked for a whole summer through the French countryside and the Italian lakes and one evening under a full moon in the Black Forest swore eternal fidelity to each other. That was in October. Back in Paris she decided to look for work. She never wanted to return to South Africa. For three weeks from early morning till after dark she went begging for a job at one address after the other. And at last found one. It was eleven o'clock in the morning. She took the metro and from Saint-Germain she ran through the first snow of winter and up the dark staircase to the green door at the top. There was a groaning, moaning, massively fat woman lying in her bed, dressed in a pair of blood-red socks, her feet high in the air and spread wide and Ulrich scrabbling between her legs like a blue fly fighting for its life in the all-engorging clasp of a gigantic carrion flower.

Julia had told me about Ulrich Neumann before. And that she'd caught him with another woman and that that had been the end of the affair and the end of her year of wandering in Europe. That evening in the deckchair she shared the horror of the moment with me for the first time. "I just stood and stared in that doorway. I couldn't believe what I was seeing. I could not utter a single sound. And they were so engrossed and making such a racket that they didn't notice me. There was half a carton of milk on the little table next to the door. I threw the milk at them. And... the rest I've still not actually managed to believe. He looked over his shoulder, saw that it was me, got up and put on his pants and took his shirt and shoes and walked past me without saying anything or looking at me. And the woman just remained lying like that. She lit a cigarette and lay there looking at me as if she thought I might also want a turn."

After that we didn't speak again. I sat looking at the stars, trying to forget about Ulrich Neumann.

I must have dozed off for a while, because at some point she was no longer next to me and the living room was dark, but when I went in there, an almost burnt-out candle was smouldering on the table and there were a blanket and a pillow on the couch. She was lying curled up in her little hollow single bed, her fists balled in front of her face.

That was at two o'clock in the morning. There were still voices around the hospital – querulous children, people calling out to each other. I sat with her on the bed for a while and later went to sleep on the couch. When I woke up, she was gone.

She was not at the clinic either. Vukile wanted to know from me where she was. I went to look outside. There were visibly more people in the yard than on the previous afternoon.

It was only after sunrise, by which time everybody was searching for her, that I found her in the church, on her knees by one of the back pews. I was sure she was asleep; her chest and cheek were resting on her folded arms. But when I touched her – I wanted to make sure, because I wanted to say goodbye before leaving – her hand was ready, as if she'd been expecting me, tired but poised to reject me.

Something of this seemed familiar. As if I'd seen her like this before. Only days later did I recall the story of her father and P.W. Botha. It had ended with just as much anger and grief before the altar.

I misled myself, that morning, when I struggled in my maltreated bakkie over the smooth grey shingle of the river, on my way home at last, when I thought: she deserves her solitude.

THREE

The mousy little girl that I used to take to church on Sunday evenings in my first term at university said that Brand de la Rey sounded like some hero from a storybook. I always remembered it because even then I thought it was bloody ironic. I was not cast in the heroic mould. At no stage of my life was I in any respect anything exceptional. From childhood I was a loner who consorted more comfortably with books than with people. My father's little study was filled with books on South African history and anthropology, travelogues, handwritten diaries of ancestors, photo albums and framed portraits of staunch uncles and aunts who united my family and history in a single narrative. It was understandable that my interest should be piqued. I'd read and reread all the diaries as early as in primary school, and in almost every one of the history books on the Boer War and the Rebellion and the National Party there were marginalia in my father's neat slanting handwriting, saying this was Grandpa Piet here and Ma's Uncle Ferdinand there and Aunt Lilly's brother Gert and Great-grandfather Andries's cousin Willem that was written about here. I got the feeling sometimes, when reading the diaries and history books, that I was in a sense the outcome of all those histories. If the story of the Afrikaners was one very long sentence full of commas and dashes, full of redundant adjectives and parentheses and ambiguous word choices, then I was the full stop at the end of that sentence. The full stop or the question mark.

Many of those names from my prehistory were the names of heroes and freedom fighters and pioneers and warriors. All of them were lonely figures. It lent romantic allure to the idea of being a loner.

I was saddled with the name, with the urge to make a difference, a longing for something beyond the horizon, a sequestered youth, a distrust of my fellow man – but nothing of the warrior or the pioneer or the hero. The distrust may have been unnecessary, but it was understandable. If the old tale of political betrayal was not merely something you read about, but the fate of your own family, then you don't just shrug it off. And if on one fine Wednesday your mother just isn't around any more and after months of enquiring and entreating you were told that she'd taken the high road with the biographer of your famous grandfather, distrust of your fellow man and prejudice against the heroes of the past inexorably become part of your mental make-up.

Very few of the paths on which I ventured had been chosen by me of my own free will. They tended to be alternative routes that willy-nilly led me to alternative destinations. I enrolled for a degree in zoology and botany because I hadn't been accepted as an engineering student. I enrolled for a Master's degree because after my Honours I couldn't find a job anywhere. I got embroiled in the relationship with Kristi because nothing else seemed to want to happen. I ended up in the bush because I was the only applicant for the job and because only someone who really wanted to put distance between himself and Kristi would have considered such a job and such a service contract.

My research project was made possible by a donation from the Rembrandt Group and the International Foundation for Nature Conservation, and was administered by the University of Cape Town's Faculty of Natural Science.

My area of interest was selected for me by my supervisor, Professor Maxwell Stokes. The initial brief was that I would collect data, over as broad a spectrum as was practically possible, on the feeding and reproductive behaviour of mammals in a region without any human population or interference like power cables, canals, reservoirs, railways or roads. To render the research in any way significant, the area had to measure at least two thousand square kilometres and contain a wide variety of mammals and types of habitat, and my observations had to extend over at least five years and be constantly correlated against existing data recorded in agricultural areas, sparsely populated regions and national parks. In time I broadened my brief myself and started working on the role of magnetite microcrystals in the sense of direction of bees, birds and certain types of fresh-water fish. That brought me to the fresh-water polyp. And in time to a whole heap of other things.

Back then, when I moved into the lath-and-clay house in the kloof, I thought I was really settling in the middle of nowhere; in the heart of the bundu – I'm never ever going to see another soul. You had to spend some time there to realize that you weren't alone – you could be lonely much of the time, but never alone. The place where you seek out solitude because of or in spite of your own make-up, that's where you'll come across the lonely ones.

Strydom was one of the few who ever visited. If visit is really the right word for his odd appearances and disappearances: Strydom sometimes dropped in. And sometimes Mills and sometimes de Gaspri. But Mills you could hardly count and Tito de Gaspri called in rather than visited. Once a month he bumped up the kloof in his asthmatic, constipated old Caball to come and deliver supplies. Mostly I was not at home; but even when I was, de Gaspri would unload his freight, drink a mug of water or on a hot day perhaps a beer, and be on his way again.

Mills never came to visit. Where he was going to or where he'd come from, one could only guess, but you would – usually in the dead of night – hear his Harley Davidson charge past at break-neck speed on the narrow twin-track forest road. And then hear him return, again long after midnight, sometimes at four o'clock in the morning, roaring down the kloof and disappearing in the distance. He'd only stop over at the house if there was something wrong with his bike or with himself. One night he turned up, sick to death, and lay delirious with fever for four days on the couch in the sitting room. The fifth afternoon, when Vusi and I got home, he was gone. With a note on the kitchen table that said *Thanx for the hospitality. Feeling better. Must go. Jock Mills.* For two months not a sign of him; then late one afternoon he thundered past in the bush and that same night he roared down the kloof again and was gone.

He was a pilot by profession without a plane. The Piper Cub that he'd had, Vukile said, he'd more or less literally drunk away from under his backside. And alcohol, he liked to explain, was the only medicine left to combat his recurring bouts of malaria.

The story that he was constructing an aeroplane somewhere in the bush was one of the many improbable and often far-fetched rumours circulating in the bush. The reason most of us distrusted Mills was that so many of his stories sounded a bit contrived. One was inclined to think that he was imagining things or embroidering the truth. Later I had to admit that I needn't have been so sceptical. Jock Mills just had a way of attracting unusual situations.

Strydom was something else again. A prospector of some kind or other, we thought initially, with a little hammer dangling from his belt and a magnifying glass in his shirt pocket. Consumptively thin and scorched black by the sun; his face just about invisible behind his rampant beard and mop of hair and patched thick-lensed glasses with a cracked left lens.

Strydom. Nobody ever asked for his first name and he never supplied it of his own accord. In all probability for him even his surname provided too much of a hold on his retiring and cautious existence.

With his way of walking stooped over forward, eyes always fixed on the ground, spectacles slipping down over his beard, he was like a question mark walking from rock to rock, always tapping away with his little hammer, spitting and licking, rubbing and collecting. His pockets were usually sagging with stone samples, and his pants inclined, like his spectacles, to slip down. His worn-out bakkie with the home-made canvas canopy was a crow's nest of dirty clothes and cans of petrol and tools and ragged books and cooking utensils.

Apart from rocks he also knew about birds and stars and music and machines and bricklaying and carpentry. He was the one who regularly had to fix the mission station's wonky generator and decrepit water pump, and he and Vusi built my clay-and-lath house in the kloof.

When I arrived home from the mission station the morning after Julia and Sister Roma's mealie-meal expedition, Strydom was in the yard helping Vusi with the back door. Apparently the door had dropped out of the wall for a second time and he was struggling to contrive a whole new back wall. Although once again struggle is not the right word, because everything Strydom did, he did as slowly as he did it thoroughly. You always got the impression, while he was winching a pump out of a borehole or examining a rock or building a wall, that he had more time than the task required.

The whole back wall had been broken out and they were digging a deep trench to sink the new wall into the ground.

"Why rebuild the whole wall?" I wanted to know. You always had the problem, in talking to him, that you shied away from addressing him directly. You could easily say Jan or Gert or Piet, but to call him by his surname implied a distance that you didn't intend. "I thought it was just the door that had come unstuck."

"Was stupid clay. Crumbly. Doesn't stick. Whole wall full of stupid cracks. Would just have carried on falling out. Laths in any case eaten up by the stupid ants."

Strydom was quite content not to address anybody directly. The addiction to first names probably figured to him as an excessive show of brotherliness without which he could get by very nicely.

There was only one way of pinning Strydom down. He was, by his own testimony, a teetotaller – but a little glass of muscadel even in his grumpiest moods was always acceptable. And the little glass of muscadel always led to a second and a third. After the first glass he would start uttering full sentences; after the second his defences were down; after the third he was lost to the world. I soon learnt never to offer him the third. He would fall into a turbulent sleep right there in his seat, disappear into thin air before daybreak and avoid you like the plague for months for fear that he might have said too much. Not that he ever did. At any rate not before it was too late, and then it was in any case not the fault of the wine.

We had gone to fetch clay down by the Bápe and to cut a load of laths in the kloof. Strydom was walking in front up a slight incline and into a stand of young bushwillows. His little hand axe was as light as a feather and razor-sharp. Just one chop and the lath would drop to the ground. Vusi and I came after and hacked off the tops and tied the bundles together with strings of bark. All the while Strydom said nothing. Only when everything had been loaded and we were passing rope to Vusi to secure the load did Strydom take off his patched specs and wipe the uncracked glass clean with his thumb. "So there, that's buggered up the bloody environment again." Which was more or less the longest full sentence that he'd up to then ever managed without wine.

I knew it was a good-humoured jibe in my direction – and only a moment later realized that it was more than a good-humoured jibe: Strydom knew about the tension between me and Julia.

Later that afternoon, with the back wall more or less reconstituted and Strydom remarkably clean after an exuberant shower under the tap in the reed enclosure, he was ready to hit the road.

"But why now?"

"It's late."

"Exactly. It's almost dark."

"Why I say."

"Sleep here. It's better than in the back in that canvas tent. Vusi is preparing food already."

"Long way."

"You don't travel at night. Not on these bush tracks."

"Do it all the time."

"I've chilled some wine."

He hesitated for a moment, turned his face so that he could look past the crack in the spectacle lens and held up an index finger. "One glass."

"One glass."

That was the first evening that the baboons were inquisitive enough to come into the yard.

A few of the biggest ones that Vusi and I had got to know in the Bápe had developed a habit of sometimes in the late afternoon coming to settle in the trees near the yard to see what we were up to. The troop leader, the big one, the one we'd baptized Malume, was always part of the group. He'd come closer than the others, but never all the way into the yard; and he'd get furious if one of his little troop ventured closer than he. He had a way of looking at me as if he expected something from me. Not food. I forbade Vusi to feed them, but the one time that I myself weakened and chucked a banana at the leader, he ignored it, and snarled away the others when they wanted to go and investigate. Every afternoon that he turned up, Malume sat in the same fork of the same tree gazing at me as if expecting a sign from me, a gesture, a message that would change everything. Sometimes I would go up to him, once to within three metres of him; he didn't clear off; he sat looking me in the eye as if expecting me now, at last, to speak the word for which he'd been waiting for so long. At times Malume reminded me of what Eugène Marais called "the dark continent of animal behaviour". That was the continent that most of all I would have liked to explore, but as yet I was much too inexperienced a traveller.

That evening the baboons were later than usual. Normally they'd arrive an hour before dark and clear off after half an hour so that they could reach their sleeping quarters before dark. That evening they arrived just before dark. And stayed. Malume sat in his usual place looking at us. But not as motionlessly as usual. Something had upset him. He got out of the tree and eventually ventured all the way into the yard, half-heartedly, inquisitively, almost indignantly.

"What's the creature looking at me like that for?" Strydom asked as the baboon came closer and closer.

It was clear that Malume was taking no notice of me; his attention was fixed on Strydom. It was as if the animal saw him as an impostor and was trying to drive him off. Later I had reason to wonder whether it hadn't been curiosity rather than hostility.

Then Vusi decided that it might just be time to bring out the lanterns.

Strydom was keeping the baboon in focus in his spectacle lenses all the while. "He doesn't like me."

"That's just his nature, a bit cock-of-the-walk."

"That's odd. Stupid things have a way of eyeing you as if they're looking at you from some other era."

Darkness fell on the narrow little front stoep before Vusi could bring out the lanterns. One moment it was a little yard with matumi trees and leadwood and round-leaved kiaat – then just a row of crouching shadows – then blind darkness and silence, with a single firefly bobbing about as if taken unawares by the night.

Vusi's lanterns made Malume and his little troop clear off. But it was too late to reach the kloof and we heard them all evening in the kiaat copse across the way from the house coughing and protesting, ill at ease and clearly anxious.

With the lanterns came the wine. I poured two glasses and passed one across the little cane table to Strydom. He took the glass and held it up against the lantern light and examined it and nodded. "So."

"Cheers."

There wasn't really any need to talk. It simply wasn't that kind of evening. We just sat gazing into the darkness as if it would bring us some unforeseen insight without which we'd had to muddle through up to then. Even when Vusi came to squat in the front door later, his back against the door frame and elbows on his knees as was his wont, it didn't spark any conversation. But it bothered no one in the least. In the bush talking is the first bad habit you shed. Silence later becomes a way of reaching out to each other.

There was nevertheless always the temptation, on such evenings, to ask him about himself. Perhaps because no one had actually got round to it, there were even more rumours about him than about Mills. That he was a palaeontologist searching for the missing link was the most interesting of the speculations. But there were others. That he was actually a geologist and the owner of lots of tin mines all over the country. That his wife had left him for his best friend and that he'd then become a bush vagrant. That he could read people's minds. That he was on the run from the police. Jock Mills was alleged to have heard somewhere that he was a dangerous psychopath. I was more or less convinced that nothing of the sort was true; he was probably just a prospector following a dream.

And yet: the mind-reading story at times seemed as if it might just have some truth to it. He would without prompting, while you were wondering whether the man didn't perhaps need a shower, say out of the blue: "Yes, a bit of water on my body might just be a good thing."

Julia had been hovering about in my thoughts all day. I couldn't forget her eyes. That morning, just before I left, she'd stood in front of me for quite a while gazing at her hands. I could see her turning things over, wanting to talk and then having second thoughts. When at last she'd looked up at me, there was such a confusion of emotions on her face that I couldn't make out what I was supposed to read there.

"I have sometimes wondered," Strydom was suddenly saying from out of the darkness, "whether you shouldn't just go and fetch her and marry her."

"Who?"

"The nun."

"Julia?"

"Yes."

I said nothing.

"The thing about people is, it's a long road to travel."

"Yes?" I asked when he seemed to have done talking. But that was the end of his story.

There were now four or five fireflies hovering to and fro in the yard like floating lanterns. We watched the fireflies and waited for time to pass.

In the kitchen, later, by the light of another two lanterns, Strydom tried to hide his empty wine glass behind the meat dish, but when I took it and refilled it, he raised no objection. He picked it up, held it against the light, and nodded. "So."

As usual Vusi had declined to eat at the table. When he and I were alone and were eating our road rations in the veld or just on our laps on the back stoep, he would still be up to it. But as soon as there was somebody else present and we sat down to the table, he would dish his food and go and eat on his own in his room.

Strydom sat pecking and picking at his food as if he weren't hungry.

"What I'm trying to say, is that people just do their own thing in their own way. Like this morning in the bushwillows. You just hear one person chopping here, another chopping there."

Coming from Strydom, these few sentences were verging on loquaciousness. Because it was early in the evening and his second glass of wine was barely touched. He looked up at me as if expecting a reaction. Something must have given him pause, because he considered for a while and shook his head and tasted his wine.

"It's true what you're saying. I suppose one should take more trouble to reach other people."

"I'm not talking about visiting. I'm talking about understanding. You walk halfway to hell to somebody else, only to find nobody at home." He'd finished his plate of food and was halfway through his second glass when he resumed his discourse with a single sentence. "Especially the women."

Because my thoughts were once again straying in Julia's direction, I looked up half-perturbed. "Why so?"

Strydom had a way of twisting his head left and right in order to see better through his glasses. He would aim left and right, move forward and back, in order to align an intact section of the left or right lens with whatever he wanted to examine. He was once again doing this. He wanted to get a decent look at me. He had clearly not grasped the reason for my question and wanted to make sure that I was being serious.

"You're supposed to know about the women," he said.

"Not much."

Strydom's reply was to down the rest of his glass in one gulp. "And I always thought," he said quite a bit later, as a kind of after-thought, "I thought you were with that nun morning and night."

"She's not a nun. She's a nurse."

"She was a nun."

"Not for too long."

"She doesn't strike me as someone who could take it for too long." The thing with him and liquor was that each drink squared the effect of the alcohol. One glass was one glass. But two was like four. Three was like nine.

"I was sitting looking at the stupid fireflies just now outside and I thought, it's like the women. Have you ever tried to catch a firefly? You grab over there where the light is shining and you're left with a handful of darkness."

"Not all of them."

"All of them."

He was at the point where the guard on his mouth was starting to abdicate. I decided that tonight was the night not to offer him a third glass; he had to talk.

"So you know about the women?"

"Know, yes. Not understand. I understand nothing. I know. As you know next morning about the hangover. That stupid taste in the mouth and the thirst and the headache. You understand nothing that happened. You remember that the beginning was pleasant and you wanted more. Of the rest you understand nothing, because you remember nothing. All you know is the stupid taste in your mouth."

"Is it really always like that?"

"Depends on your constitution I suppose. Do you love her?"

"Who?"

"The nun."

"I suppose I do."

"Hm." He gripped his glass between three lean fingers and slid it across the table next to the wine bottle. "Yes, well." And when I seemed to be ignoring the glass, he took the bottle and poured for himself.

There was a moth around the lanterns – a large, lazy moth that floated flapping from light to light looking for an entry. Strydom watched the moth, his head aiming all the time to get it in focus. Then he picked up his glass and held it to the light and nodded. "So."

"You were married?"

I dropped the question into the dead silence, very tentatively, as one moves a pawn of which you're not sure. Perhaps I spoke too softly, or perhaps Strydom decided not to hear the question. He just sat motionlessly staring out in front of him, without batting an eyelid. When at last he started talking, it was as if resuming a conversation that he'd been having for a considerable time. "Eden was somewhere in the Rift Valley." He looked up into the darkness, sipped at his wine, and looked for me in the lens of his glasses. "We arrived there with memories of pain. With a fear of darkness. With a vague premonition of something. We left the valley with the knowledge of good and evil. The ability to discriminate. A first sighting of the unknown. A stupid unrealizable yearning."

The night was a house with a yard, a forest without sound, and at the same time an immeasurable vacuum around us; a primeval darkness in which everything stopped dead.

Later Strydom's glass was empty and we neither of us thought to refill it.

I went and put the kettle on for coffee. I could hear that Vusi had gone to his room already – as always, this time of night, fiddling with his transistor, looking for a bit of short-wave music from Zanzibar or Dar es Salaam. I latched the back door. When I got back, Strydom was fast asleep face-down on the table.

2

Vukile Khumalo called me the next morning just after daybreak to hear how Vusi was responding to his pills. "He's still alive, thanks, Vukile." First the little cackle. "No, really, brother. I'm worried about him."

"It's going well. He's fit as a fiddle." I chose not to breathe a word about Gwaja's root muti. "How are things there?"

"Madhouse. We counted them last night. Hundred and forty something."

"So what are you going to do?"

"Ask Julia. She's standing next to me."

"I don't think she wants to talk to me."

"Why not?" Suddenly, there was Julia's voice. "I was the one who asked him to call you."

"Morning, Julia."

"Hello…" There was the same hesitant tailing-off to her voice as the previous day, as if everything she said was a question that remained unasked.

"You must be tired."

"Nothing that a good night's sleep won't fix. Nobody is getting any sleep."

"You should take turns."

"We do take turns. But it's… difficult to sleep…"

"I wish you could come here for a few days."

There was a brief silence. "When are you coming again?"

"I don't know yet. Strydom is here. Why?"

She hesitated again. As if she wanted to say something and couldn't get it said. Previously it had always been good to know that we could say anything to each other by radio, because nobody at the station or within listening range of our feeble little transmitters could understand Afrikaans. But that morning it was as if she suspected all the time that somebody was listening in.

"You must come, please. When you can. We need help. This thing is getting out of hand."

"I know. What kind of help do you have in mind?"

"Vukile wants to talk to you again."

"Julia?"

"No, it's me, brother. Listen, have you ever shot a hippo?"

"No. Why?"

"Will you shoot one for us?"

"Absolutely not!"

Apparently there was an old rogue bull higher up next to the river that was running amok. He'd invaded several settlements the previous few nights and got at the people's stores of mealies. But during the day there was no trace of him.

"Grass is scarce. He must be hungry."

"*Ja*, but dammit – he's dangerous!"

"It's probably an old bull who can't walk far enough to look for food."

"Then surely you won't mind shooting it."

"I'll come and have a look next time I come in that direction," was all that I would promise. "But I'm not going to shoot him. Let me know when you've tracked him down."

"Julia wants to speak to you."

And then her voice was there again. "Brand, we can feed these people for a week on the meat of that animal."

"I know. But slaughter Gwaja's goats first."

"All hell broke loose here today. The people got stuck into his herd and cut the throats of seven. Vukile had to give him a pill to get him to calm down."

"Then there'll be a good fifty or so left."

"No! Every day a few of them die. I think he's only got ten or twelve left."

"He's a blessed man."

"Are you well?"

"Yes, thanks."

"We must talk."

"Hell, Julia, that's all we ever do. We must start talking less."

"And then what?"

"I don't know. But that's all we ever do. We just talk non-stop. And nothing gets said."

"What I said last night wasn't exactly what I meant. All I meant was that it doesn't matter what *I* think or feel, the circumstances matter more."

"For ever and ever?"

"They're looking for me back there, Brand. We'll talk again."
Then the radio went dead.

Vusi, still half-asleep and clearly not in a good mood, was getting the kettle on the boil. The kitchen smelt of woodsmoke and freshly ground coffee and damp clay.

Strydom was no longer in the living room on the couch where I'd covered him with a blanket the previous night. The blanket was neatly folded on the little plank chest next to the window. The lantern was out and the glass chimney lifted.

I went outside and breathed in the fresh air a few times. There was a spot of vomit by the outside tap.

Strydom's bakkie was gone.

3

The outside room where I kept my apparatus and books and results was the sturdiest structure around. It was made of raw brick and cement, with steel-framed windows and a corrugated-iron roof to make it a bit more fire-resistant. Inside there was a desk full of loose papers, two big baboon skulls and a typewriter; there was a chair, a row of bookshelves with books and files, a steel cabinet, a washbasin and tap, and an almighty big home-made table under an oilcloth. On the table was a row of flasks with chemicals and formalin, a spirit burner, a pipette holder and a little rack with round-bottom flasks and burettes. In a cupboard with glass doors of which almost every pane had been broken on the long trek through the bundu were dry butterflies, the reconstituted skeletons of lizards and birds, a cisticola nest with eggs and all sorts of dung beetles, river crabs and a giant rock-lizard skull. Like the glass-doored cupboard and the desk and the bookshelves, the walls were over-full; hung and pasted over with tables, graphs, photos, maps, cuttings, sketches, pressed leaves, feathers, bones and cured snakeskins.

Nobody was ever allowed into the outside room. Not even Vusi. I dusted and swept and tidied the place myself. My first major tiff with Julia was exactly because I wouldn't show her the place. "I trust Vusi with my life, but I don't allow him even to sweep the place. How would I explain to him that I allow you in there?"

"What... why? Are you scared we'll break the place down? Are you scared we'll steal something?"

"It's a workplace, Julia, not a gathering place. All it takes is for someone to touch something by accident and—"

"Ah, excuse me, yes, I'd forgotten I'm a naughty child who can't keep her hands to herself."

Vusi, in his turn, was convinced that I occupied myself at night with all sorts of secret rituals and sacrifices and witchcraft. And it was Vusi's tales about this that caused the people across the river to stand in awe of me, sometimes referring to me as the white *umthakathi*.

Sometimes, especially after Julia's snide response, I said to myself that perhaps I was overly protective of the outside room. But even I, who always moved about so cautiously when I was there, once undid a whole day's patient and delicate reconstruction of the skeleton of a rare little tree salamander with one negligent hand gesture.

Vusi was prohibited from entering the outside room for all kinds of practical reasons, but by the same token I would never dream of entering Vusi's bedroom. From the very first day he'd been rather possessive of his quarters. It was always locked and the outside window was covered up with newspaper. "For the spirits," he explained, "that walk with the chameleon."

But the morning when I had to carry a delirious Vusi out to the bakkie to take him to hospital, it wasn't just his shivering fit and his eyes rolling back in his head and his foaming mouth that gave me a fright – it was also his room. Because except for the books and apparatus it was almost a replica of my own workplace. The end was perhaps totally different, but the means were the same: in the feeble light of the lantern I could discern skulls and feathers and dassie hides and calabashes everywhere, and also: porcupine quills and lala seeds and a small knucklebone. And with a sudden cold shiver I remembered many nights of waking up to a voice in the stoep room. At first I thought it was the radio, but once when I was going to complain about the noise I heard that it was Vusi talking to himself... or to some invisible other presence. I asked him about this just once and never again. Because Vusi ignored the question as if it had never been asked.

Back from hospital, more or less cured of whatever had ailed him, I carried his bag for him as far as the back stoep, took the key to the padlock out of my pocket and put it into his hand. Our eyes met squarely for a moment, and that was enough. I could see that Vusi knew I hadn't been inside his room again.

With Strydom now gone, I could go and unlock the outside room and start working. There was more than a week's worth of loose notes that I had to marshal and a half-completed article that I was writing and that I wanted de Gaspri to post for me at the end of the month. Vusi left on foot to the matumi forest in the kloof to check if the honeyguides had moved into the nest with imitation eggs.

Because the corrugated-iron roof was very hot in summer, I always left the door and windows wide open when I worked in the outside room by day – sometimes with surprising consequences. A Namaqua canary that occurred exclusively in the north-west of the country, *Serinus atrogularis*, flew in by the door one day and settled on the bookshelf, bewildered. And one late-autumn afternoon a big spitting rinkhals suddenly reared up cheekily in fighting fettle right next to my desk.

The man entered just as quietly as the rinkhals. He could have been there for a long time, but I hadn't noticed anything. The sound could at first have passed for that of a bird or an insect in the yard outside. It had probably been carrying on for a while, but it was so dehumanized that I gave no heed to it. It was not the sound but the smell that eventually caught my attention: a mixture of sweat and tobacco and the bittersweet fume of putrescence. I looked up from my work and out of the window, but there was nothing out of the ordinary to be seen outside. It was a barren, white morning vibrating with light and cicadas. It was only when I slapped at a fly that was trying to settle on my face that my eye caught something right where I'd least expected it.

The man was squatting on his haunches to the right of my desk. Except for a rag of dirty hide around his middle and a thin string of white beads around his neck he was naked. His eyes were half shut and around his mouth and nose a swarm of flies had caked of which he seemed unaware. He was so emaciated that you could see his skeleton under the skin – skull and shoulder blades and finger bones and ribs only just covered by the greyish membrane that must have once been skin. The man tried to open his eyes but could not. He sat rocking on his heels as if he was going to fall over. The more he tried to open his eyes, the more the pupils rolled back, showing only the white balls in the deep eye sockets. But it was as if the man was holding me in his stare right through the thin quivering eyelids.

Only later that day did I realize that I'd probably been given a greater fright by the man's unexpected presence than by the rinkhals. Because it took me ten or twelve seconds to utter a single word.

"*Ufunani?*" (What do you want?)

The man's eyes went still as if he was trying to listen.

"*Ubani whena? Uphumapi?*" (Who are you? Where are you from?) It looked as if the man was trying to get to his feet. He fell forward with his head against the desk, and remained lying just like that.

"*Ufunani?*" I could find nothing else to say. I knew damned well what the man wanted, but for the time being I was just too bewildered to think clearly.

I picked him up and held him in my arms like a child. He was terrifyingly light. I was on my way out with him. The man opened his eyes and I could see his grey-black pupils. We looked each other in the eye uncertainly and the man opened his mouth and something emerged from his mouth – with the drool something appeared between his lips, a whitish thing, a dumb tongue. A word – a soft, murmured, inaudible word.

I couldn't make out the word. I turned my ear to the man's mouth.

"*Utsini?*" (What are you saying?)

"*Ngilambile.*" (I am hungry.)

His head drooped down on my chest. The grey-black eyes turned quite grey and then went blind.

Vusi and I buried him by lantern light that evening. And that was the first grave in the kloof.

FOUR

I

The next morning, after a long altercation on the radio, Julia eventually persuaded me at least just to have a look at why the hippo was behaving so oddly, and for safety's sake to bring along my rifle. She had a rifle of her own that she had inherited from her father; the rifle was one of the few heirlooms small enough to take with her. It was a triple-two and far too light for shooting a hippo. She knew this and won the argument that morning only because she threatened to go and shoot the animal herself with her rifle.

She would never admit it, but it was probably a case of like father like daughter. They were both equally bloody-minded. Tielman Krige had been a Member of Parliament and one of P.W.'s confidants, and just about never at home. That may have been the reason why she and her father never learnt to get along with each other, except in that year or so in high school when Julia brandished the old Transvaal flag so patriotically. Although even then she deemed it necessary to question everything that Tielman said about politics, and to accept it only when she heard it on television being proclaimed by the State President as well.

It was P.W.'s hullabaloo about the brown minister who'd been so cheeky as to swim on a beach designated for whites only that had made her wonder for the first time. After that she started doubting more and more things. She heard less and less of what P.W. was saying and couldn't look past his threatening index finger, until that finger later became an obscene, throbbing organ thrusting up all over the country's television screens. She discussed it with her father, and this issued in their last great barney, which became so extreme that she fled from the house. Her father and the police found her the next morning a kilometre from home asleep in front of the altar of a little Catholic church. "Why here of all places?" Tielman demanded indignantly. "In a Catholic church!"

"Why not, Pa?"

"My house is full of books on the Roman peril and you ask me why not!"

A few years later when the convent's gates clanged shut behind her, she remembered her father's words. And suddenly, for the first time in a long while, felt safe. She was yet to discover that you take yourself and your past with you everywhere, and that the tables of all that is to come have been set a long time ago.

That day with the hippo it was still the same headstrong Julia who obliged me to clean and oil the barrel of my dusty rifle and to calibrate the sights.

Vukile let me know that they'd tracked the hippo down to about two kilometres downstream. He was crippled and very aggressive. The pool in the river that he'd appropriated for himself was the last remaining washing and watering hole of quite a few families.

It was five o'clock in the afternoon and Vusi was making tallies next to the Bápe. I went to pick him up.

"*Siyakuphi?*" he asked.

I told him about the hippo.

"Are you going to shoot him?"

"Only if he's dangerous."

Vusi seldom smiled. And even when he did, it was a smile that started with his mouth and never reached his eyes. He was a small, slender man with a shaven head and an aquiline nose and eyes the colour of smoke-blackened lantern glass. Uncanny eyes that often while he was talking to you would be looking at something somewhere between the two of you where there was nothing.

"Are you going to give his meat to the people?"

"Yes, Vusi."

I realized that afternoon that, given adequate reason, his eyes could laugh after all.

We'd have to shoot the hippo before sunset if shooting was unavoidable. In the dark it would be much more difficult and certainly more dangerous.

We reached Mbabala just after six.

The place was just about unrecognizable. There were now leaf-and-branch shelters around the hospital and round the back of the church and the few dwellings, even among the banana trees on both sides of the road. Or what had remained of the bananas. Because most of the leaves had been stripped and packed over the shelters for shade. Even the few papaya trees had been pushed over to get at the leaves. When I pulled up, five, six reed-thin people in rags crowded around the bakkie begging for food. One of them was a girl of probably not more than twelve with an inflamed scar on her cheek. One of the few whose name I got to know later. Nandi. At first I thought she was dancing for a handout, as children sometimes do next to the main roads, but she was far too weak for that – she was simply trying to keep her balance. It was the slow, almost comical, macabre dance of death of a girl of twelve hoping we were bringing her salvation. She stretched out her hand to me and when I took it, she couldn't believe that there was nothing in my hand except her own.

Others were trying to clamber into the back of the bakkie to get at the tin trunk that was always locked to the roll bar.

If the mission station was not exactly what it had been, the same could be said of Julia and the nuns. They were visibly run-down and overwrought. Sister Erdmann, wax-pale and sweat-drenched and crumpled, almost walked over me without greeting me, and to judge by the voice it was definitely Sister Roma who was totally losing her temper somewhere in the courtyard.

Julia held me and leant her head against my chest and just stood there like that, for quite a while. "I'm glad you're here."

"I would have been much gladder if I hadn't had to come and shoot a hippo."

"That animal is suffering. You'll see. It looks as if he's got a wire around his front paw. He can't walk any more."

"Must be a snare. They set the things for the few kudus that still come to drink."

"Come, I'll go and show you."

"You're not going along."

"I'm the only one who knows where he is. I went to look for him this morning."

"On foot?"

"That was all I had."

"You're mad, Julia!"

"As I was saying."

"Just give me directions. Vusi's going with me."

"We don't have much daylight left. We'll have to get going." I got Julia to drive. Vusi and Gwaja and I were in the back.

It always surprised me to see how capably she did everything. Whether treating a wound or feeding a baby or driving a bakkie in the bush, it was always with the steady hand of someone who knew exactly what she was doing. We crossed a stretch of veld that I wouldn't have tackled sight unseen – shrubs higher than the canopy of the bakkie hardly broke her speed. Invisible tree trunks and dongas and patches of deep sand were scraped past as if she'd been informed in advance that she would emerge unscathed at the other end. There'd be no use in teaching her to drive carefully, because that was how she had always lived her life.

The hippo was lying on his left side among the reeds in a small pool. The sun had gone down, but it was still light enough to see, at a distance of forty metres, that the right foot was more than twice its normal size. Through the binoculars one could see the white flesh just above the toes protruding from under the split-open hide. It was an exceptionally large hippo.

When I got off the back of the bakkie, the animal lifted its head and started struggling to its feet. He was a few metres from the pool and I knew I had to shoot before he could enter the water. Anything other than a headshot would have no effect – it would just cause more pain and aggression. But the hippo did not flee into the water. It charged, if one could describe his stumbling, falling advance as a charge. There were young waterberry trees and reeds and bulrushes in the way and the light was already too dim to take aim really carefully.

I just fired. But I had to fire a second and a third time before the beast eventually fell down for the last time.

The length of steel wire around his foot was so covered in swelling that we couldn't see it at all – only the end that had snapped still stuck out from the half-rotten wound.

The carcass was even bigger than the living animal had seemed – probably something in the region of two thousand kilograms. It would take a few men several hours to skin it and cut the meat into transportable chunks.

I knew we'd have to do it that night, otherwise there'd be only bones left the next morning. I tried to concentrate on the work ahead and tried very hard not to think of the final bullet that had stopped the animal's charge in its tracks.

The hippo's hide was grey with caked mud. It had obviously not ventured into the water for a long time. Julia remained standing at a distance. She probably knew very well what would happen if she had to take a close look at that prehistoric beast's lifeless innocence. She wasn't going to trip herself up.

It was the second-to-last day of January in that third year of drought. It was the first time in the seven years of my sojourn in the bundu that I'd killed something. And something told me, contrary to my sacred intention, that it would not be the last.

2

We worked through the night. Julia fetched storm lanterns and saws and hatchets and butcher's knives, and Vusi and Gwaja and I had to skin and cut up the meat. In the hissing light of the storm lanterns there was an almost excessive urgency to everything we did; something almost demoniac in the sweating faces and grabbing hands sawing and cutting and chopping among the mosquitoes and nocturnal moths and green insects at the plenitude of a time-less creature with its thick banks of flesh and white blubber – two kilometres from a multitude of starving people lying with rolled-back eyes under their branch shelters waiting for daybreak and the inexorable ultimate darkness.

We took turns at slaughtering. It took almost half an hour to chop through the thick hide and the layer of blubber from the chest to between the hind legs, until the warm innards suddenly collapsed from out of the carcass and spilt around our hands and feet onto the grass. We cut out the lungs and the heart and the liver and dragged them up against the bank and covered them with reeds so as to ward off the insects. We sawed off the feet and head and cut the hide in strips and trimmed it and stood wondering at our own handiwork. The furious, mud-brown hippopotamus of dusk was now a motionless, pale mound of blubber and exposed nerves and pink marrow and blood.

When it was my turn to take a break, I climbed up the bank and sat up there to escape the mosquitoes. There was a veld fire to the north of us at the foot of the Ubombos, the third one that week. Previously there'd been fires every winter, usually started by light-ning, but with the drought they had gradually been getting scarcer – there was no lightning and literally not enough grass for a fire. That week's fires, I suspected, had been started by humans. Vusi had seen some people, a few weeks earlier, setting fire to banks of reeds to drive game out of the underbrush and then head off the weakest one and beat it to death with sticks.

Julia took the first load of meat back to the station at eleven o'clock and brought back hot coffee; and the second load at one o'clock. She reported that Sister Roma and her helpers had four iron cauldrons on the fire. The third and last delivery was mainly hide and bones and sinew and paws.

Vukile was in the kitchen before daybreak to prevent whole chunks of meat from being distributed. "It will kill them, Julia – please believe me, they won't be able to digest the stuff. Shred the meat and give them soup!"

She knew he was right.

They filled cauldrons and buckets and tins with soup and carried them out and fed the people, and those who could feed themselves fed themselves.

I helped till dark that evening. Vusi and Gwaja stoked the fires and cut up the meat, and Sister Erdmann and two other helpers made the soup; Julia and Roma fed the people who could no longer feed themselves.

The previous night and all that day there hadn't been time for thinking – much less for talking. Even Vukile managed somehow without his customary joviality and worked with a zeal and urgency that he seldom displayed.

At sundown Julia reported that there were two hundred and sixty-four people in the compound, almost sixty more than that morning.

Nobody had thought that Jock Mills would ever again be of any use to his fellow man. But I knew that evening that I had to get hold of him urgently.

Tito de Gaspri usually, depending on the day of the week, de-livered his supplies within the first three days of the month. But if the first fell on a weekday, it was always the first.

The first of February was the next day, a Friday. Chances were ten to one that he'd bring the month's groceries that day – not only ours, those of everybody in the vicinity; and everybody in the vicinity comprised us, the mission station, the little shop at Catuane and the copper mine.

There were two people who would know where to track down Jock Mills: Strydom, but he'd probably be in hiding again for the next few weeks, and de Gaspri.

Julia had just emerged from the shower when I arrived at her place.

"I thought you'd be fast asleep by now!"

It was after nine and she'd left for home just after sundown to snatch a few hours' sleep. "Then I made the mistake of just lying down for a moment. And then I only woke up a while ago."

It was no wonder. She'd been on her feet without a break for almost forty hours.

"You must get some proper sleep for a change."

"You too."

"De Gaspri is bringing the supplies tomorrow. I must get home."

"He unloads the stuff, whether you're there or not, doesn't he?"

"How long do you think it will remain on the back stoep before it absconds?" I'd decided for the time being not to mention Jock Mills's aeroplane. Because it was a crazy idea rife with maybes and ifs and buts. But I'd seen enough the last few days to realize that I was fighting a losing battle: I'd have to help or perish along with them. Because there was no obvious solution, we'd be forced to think in more unconventional terms, and in such a framework Jock Mills miraculously came into his own.

"Will you help me if I can get these people plus all those still to arrive to the Red Cross in Durban or wherever?"

"Who says the Red Cross wants them?"

"That's not my question. If I can find a place that will care for them that is better equipped than you... will you..."

"Not than you. Than *us*. Please stop shrugging off the responsibility."

"That's exactly what I'm not doing!"

"I am sorry."

"Will you help me?"

"Of course."

"Even if it is a crazy plan?"

"If it will help the people, yes."

"Will you trust me, even if it seems like a gamble?"

"If you believe it may work, I'd be only too pleased."

"I won't know for sure that it may work until I've tried it."

"As long as it's not a gamble for you as well, I'll help you."

"Thank you."

I knew I was signing away my freedom and she was adding fine print, but I didn't expect to negotiate a more favourable contract.

But she hadn't finished. "So what's it all about?"

"I don't know yet. I'm still thinking. That's another reason why I have to get to see de Gaspri. Or Strydom." I didn't want to mention Mills's name at all.

"You can't cart off these people in de Gaspri's lorry. Not on these bad roads. Not to Durban. They'll never make it."

"I'm still thinking, Julia. I told you I'm still thinking." I shook my head. "No, not de Gaspri's lorry."

"Not Strydom's bakkie either."

"I know." The roads were too bad and it was much too far to transport them by road. The nearest railway line was at the far end of the worst section of the road. There was only one way out – an airlift.

"Then what, Brand?"

"I don't know yet. But I'm working on it."

"The government will have to help."

"The government has enough problems of its own. The drought is not only in Mozambique and Swaziland."

"Then the UN must help."

"Do you happen to have their number?"

We had a way of sending each other up. It was just a game – a dangerous kind of game in which we both participated with equal gusto. It got out of hand sometimes, but most of the time it served exactly to defuse an imminent argument.

"That may not be a joke. If I know our government, they haven't given it a thought."

"Channels, Julia. There are channels. Do you think the UN will listen to an inaudible phone call from some crazy little nurse in the bundu?"

"Not a crazy little nurse."

"You've said yourself you're crazy."

"I'll say my name is Mother Theresa."

It was at such times that I wished I could hold her to me. I knew her body would smell of rosemary and buchu. But I didn't do it. I talked. Talk was for both of us a form of avoidance of each other, a safety valve, a smokescreen. "I know you're tired and this is not the time to talk, but just tell me what it is that you wanted to discuss so urgently yesterday."

"It's no longer necessary."

"Not?"

"I wanted to show you what was happening here. Because anybody who sees it and can carry on with his life as if nothing's the matter belongs before a firing squad. But I can see you've seen enough."

It was she who suddenly held me, her cheek pressed hard against my chest. I put my arms around her body, surprised at how small she was, how narrow her back. She did not smell of buchu or rosemary – there was a whiff of almond and lukewarm water and freshly crushed peach pip. I took her head in my hands and when she looked up, there was a moment in which we both, at first hesitantly, then precipitately, started toppling towards each other from either side of a high precipice. But she turned her face away.

I've often asked myself whether my need for Julia was in any way related to Julia, or whether it was just part of my bush-bedevilled brain's hallucinations.

Father Mundt once told me, standing outside on the lawn after a game of chess that had brought us up against midnight and an empty bottle of sherry, what the bush sometimes could do to even a dedicated celibate such as he. It was a moonless night and it was drizzling softly and we stood decorously next to each other piddling with that kind of dignity of which you're capable only when you've had a tad too much to drink. Father Mundt was always very discreet and he had no truck with tittle-tattle. But it had been an exceptionally good game of chess, which he'd clinched in his favour just before midnight with a single brilliant move. We were talking about the way the bush had of sometimes infesting your head. This was before the time of Ursula Frisch – at the time he and Sister Kaiser were alone at the station. He was then a man in his early fifties and she was a good eight years older and really not very prepossessing. But he had started catching himself having all sorts of extravagant daydreams about her.

"I couldn't understand it. Because when I stand in front of her and look at her, then there's nothing for me to desire. But in the morning when I pray or in the afternoon when I'm reading or at night when I wake up, then I catch myself thinking strange things that are nothing to do with her or me, but everything to do with... yes, with what? With an immeasurable lack. And because there's no one else that I know well enough to play that role for me, she's the one who time and again comes pirouetting into this vacuum."

Father Mundt shook himself off and dropped his dress and gave a step back as if he wanted to get some distance on his recently completed handiwork. I could see the drops of rain glistening in his dark beard.

"Eventually it was every night. Because, you see, such things are complicated by the fact that day after day before sunrise you have to sit in the confessional listening to the confessions of your erotic object. And when it transpires that she's struggling, let's say, with the same problem as you, then in time you're lumbered with her daily confessions as addenda to your own daydreams. That's how I learnt to play chess. She and I both. We taught each other. Because we discovered that nothing eradicates the bush in your head as effectively as a good game of chess."

I was up against the same immeasurable lack. But Julia was a far cry from Sister Kaiser. Julia was Julia.

It was only afterwards that I started comprehending how everything that had happened to her before Mbabala was steeling her against the lack that the bush would bring to Father Mundt and Sister Kaiser and me, and to Strydom and Vusi and de Gaspri and Gwaja and Vukile and Mills, and eventually also to her.

She'd always dismissed the story of Jan Tolmay as just another episode, but I sometimes got the impression that he'd hurt her more than all the others. She'd known Ulrich Neumann in Paris, and the faraway place had perhaps made everything seem more romantic, but at one moment Jan Tolmay was on the point of marrying her and the next moment a woman she didn't know from a bar of soap phoned and said you can have him if you want him, just as long as you know that I'm six months' pregnant and he's the father. She'd by and large have preferred a blubbering Jan Tolmay begging for forgiveness to the man who on his return home that afternoon tried to shrug it all off as a misunderstanding. When at last, a month later, she started packing her suitcases one Saturday morning, he was picked up at home by a bunch of loudmouthed men for some event at Ellis Park.

"What do I do with the key?" she asked, flabbergasted, as if that were in any way the point of the matter.

"Chuck it away," he shouted as they were pulling off. "I've got a duplicate."

I don't suppose such things are just water off a duck's back.

I started piecing together the stories she told about herself and got more and more insight into her distrust. Augusta announcing out of the blue I'm not your mother; Mary Lambert sneaking into bed with her; Ulrich Neumann scrabbling like a fly in a saucer of syrup on top of a strange woman; Jan Tolmay waving gaily through the car's back window as if he were going fishing on the Vaal Dam. Everything said again and again hang on to your heart, hang on, don't trust a soul with it.

The lack was there and it was great, but the mistrust was greater.

3

De Gaspri turned up at ten o'clock in the morning with his tin of paraffin and sack of coal and mealie-meal and packets of pasta and eggs and meat and canned vegetables.

No, he didn't want to take a seat. He was in a hurry. He just wanted a glass of water. He was one of those odd, angular people whose face you don't really notice, because you're too engrossed in staring at his sharp shoulders and elbows and kneecaps.

"Tito, when last did you see Jock Mills?"

"A while now."

"You know about the plane he's fixing?"

Tito turned over his options for a while and then shrugged. "I hear them talking, yes. But I don't know."

I'd made a wager with Julia one night that she wouldn't succeed in asking Tito de Gaspri a question to which he'd give a straightforward answer. His answers were always conspicuously vague – so vague that they left one exactly none the wiser.

"Has he ever talked to you about it?"

"Not so that you'd say so."

"What kind of plane is it?"

"I don't know about planes."

"Do you know where the place is that he's working on the thing?"

"I just hear where he's travelling. I don't see in which direction."

"Perhaps Strydom knows."

"Strydom is over there somewhere." He knocked back the last bit of his mug of water and put the mug on the table on the back stoep.

"Looks like his bakkie's packed up."

"Where?"

"A little distance thataway."

"How much do you charge for your lorry, Tito? If one rents it."

"Nobody drives my lorry. Just me."

"No, you and the lorry together. How much do you charge a day?"

"Depends."

That was enough of answering questions. For one day more than enough. His vagueness regarding his fee could always be used against him later if need be.

Tito's "little distance thataway" was twenty kilometres past the turn-off to Jozini. Strydom was sitting in the back of his bakkie under the canopy, filling his pipe, his hands pitch-black with oil and his glasses slipping down low over his beard.

"Stupid diesel pipe burst. Just like that."

"How long have you been stranded here?"

"Yesterday morning. Nobody comes this way."

"Except de Gaspri."

"Stupid never stops."

"I think I may have a pipe like that at home."

We towed the bakkie home and replaced the diesel pipe. When the engine took at last, Strydom didn't even want to switch off. No, he's in a hurry. He has to go.

"Listen Strydom, switch off that thing. I have to talk to you. It's important."

"Talked a lot of shit the other evening. Must have been the stupid wine."

"Forget the other evening. Jock Mills. Do you know where he keeps that plane of his?"

"I think they call it Shabeni."

"Do you know where it is?"

"More or less."

"Will you go and show me?"

"When?"

"Now."

"No. I'm in a hurry."

"Fine, then I'll take back my diesel pipe."

We travelled in my bakkie on an overgrown twin-track road to the north-west, around Dumisane's hills and along the slope of a mountain to an open plain next to the border. An hour's drive. It must have been a twin-track road originally, but it had become overgrown; Mills's Harley had opened up here the left and there the right track as every now and again he dodged rocks and dongas and the branches of trees. Some distance into the plain the road fizzled out in what looked like an abandoned open-strip mine. The long row of overgrown portable toilets was an indication that it could have been used as an army base during the bush war. We stopped.

"It's around here somewhere now," Strydom said as he got out.

"Here's the track of the bike. That way."

In the grass, between the growth of shrubs and young thorn trees, there were bare patches everywhere with rotting army tents flattened by wind and weather, capsized tin tables, washbasins, target boards, tyres, trailers without wheels, crates, parachutes, ammunition cases and a washing line with the last remains of a few uniforms. The exodus from the camp had been a frantic, probably nocturnal operation.

Strydom was standing at a distance beckoning.

Everywhere around the camp there were flatcrown thorns. Mills's cycle track weaved through the thorn trees for two hundred metres to a stretch of open veld that had evidently once served as a landing strip about two hundred metres wide and Heaven knows how long.

And at the end of the landing strip, like a melancholy grasshopper left behind when the swarm departed, there was this plane. One hell of a thing. Probably about two storeys high and a good thirty metres long, on two high front wheels, painted grey and green, but already rusted in places.

We first stood looking at the thing from the outside. Apart from the rust there was, on the face of it, nothing wrong with the plane. It was parked on a small oil-stained concrete slab. Right under the belly of the plane was a tin table cluttered with tools and gears and strange contraptions and old liquor bottles full of black and grey and green liquid.

There was a primitive pole ladder up into the plane.

Inside was seating for probably forty people. The cockpit was dusty, but to an untrained eye it seemed fully operational. Right in the back was a hatch to a small baggage hold. And in this small hold there was a roll of blankets, a meagre little mattress, a badly worn English Bible, a notebook full of struck-through lists of spare parts and hastily drawn diagrams, a small jerrycan of water, a *Playboy*, a tin plate and a toothbrush.

We drove home.

Before sundown there was a two-hundred-litre diesel drum in the middle of the narrow bush track with a piece of cardboard on it, and in big black Koki letters a message:

Jock come see me very urgent. Brand de la Rey.

Strydom left that same evening. He was not in the mood for company. And especially not for that of Jock Mills.

4

More than a week passed without a sign of Jock. I'm a light sleeper but that week I lay reading till almost midnight every night in the hope of hearing a motorbike approaching. And then when at last I fell asleep, I was wide awake again every so often, convinced that it was the din of the Harley Davidson that had woken me. But every time there was nothing. That Friday night it was a hammering on my bedroom window and not a motorbike that woke me.

"Mr de la Rey!"

"Yes."

"Mills."

"Wait, I'm coming."

Jock Mills was a man of round about forty. A fairly well-worn forty. Lots of sun and wind and whisky.

His red hair was usually wind-blown, the skin around his eyes pale where the goggles shielded it from the sun, his lips dry and chapped, his voice remarkably sonorous for such a short and slight little man.

I lit the lamps. The stove was cold and there was no wood in the chest; I made do with the Primus for coffee.

"I got your telegram."

"Telegram?"

"Bush telegram. By drum."

"Oh yes. You drink coffee?"

"If you have nothing stronger."

"Unfortunately not."

There were a few bottles of wine and a bit of brandy in the cupboard, but after more than an hour's sleep I wasn't in the mood for a booze-up.

"I went to see your plane the other day."

Mills did not respond at once, just sat looking at me as if weighing up what he should say.

"How far is it from flying?"

"She."

"She?"

"She."

We looked each other square in the eye for a moment and reached an accord. Right. She.

"How do you know about her?"

"The bush is full of eyes."

"More stories than eyes. Everybody talks about things they know nothing about."

"Will she fly?"

"Why not?"

"When?"

"Tomorrow."

"You're going to fly her tomorrow?"

"I mean she can fly." He looked up at the roof and gulped. "Well, I think she can."

"You're not sure?"

"Everything is working that should work. I hope. I must just get the engines started."

"They haven't been… You mean they haven't run?"

"Have you ever all on your ace turned over the engine of a Dakota DC-3 by hand?"

"No."

"Try it some time."

"If somebody helped you…"

"I need batteries. The things are damned expensive and damned heavy to transport on your lap. I bought one second-hand, then it buggered off the bike on this stretch of rotten road up the mountain. My legs were raw for weeks from the acid."

"So if you could find batteries, you could fly?"

"Yip."

"What do you use for fuel?"

"Petrol."

"I know that. Which you find where?"

"I have enough."

I kept myself occupied with making coffee in an attempt to gain time. Something was telling me with ever-increasing clarity what I'd actually known from the outset: that you should think twice before undertaking anything with Jock Mills.

We were halfway through our mugs of coffee when Jock put down his mug and folded his arms. "You summoned me to interrogate me about the Dakota?"

"Yes."

"Shit!"

"Supposing your Dakota can actually fly. And supposing I can get us enough fuel. Would you be able to fly passengers in that thing?"

"What thing?"

"The Dakota."

"She's not a thing."

"Could you take passengers?"

"Why not?" He drained the dregs of his coffee and put the mug down hard on the table. "Anyway. I must go," he said in English.

Mills was actually English-speaking, but he was equally fluent in Afrikaans. I was to learn later that when he switched to English in Afrikaans company it was a sign of irritation or impatience. If, on the other hand, he switched from English to Afrikaans, it was to swear more effectively.

"More coffee?"

"No thanks. I could have been there by now."

"Coffee with brandy. I think I've got a dram left somewhere."

"Spit it out, Mr de la Rey," he said, still in English. "What's on your mind?"

The dram of brandy was considerably more than I'd remembered. It was more than half a bottle. By three o'clock that morning the bottle was empty. Jock Mills was as sober as the morning breeze and ready to fly his first consignment of Chopis to London before sunrise. "There's no point in dumping them in Durban or

Johannesburg. There's not much food left there either. We take them to London for the Brits to feed."

It was my turn to drift into uneasy slumber next to a rocking kitchen table bobbing like a marooned vessel on the open sea.

But I was not granted much time to sleep. Mills woke me up at five o'clock and at half-past five, after a cold shower and two mugs of black coffee, we were on our way. Apparently there was a trader at Jozini with a stock of reconditioned batteries at a reasonable price. Two ordinary twelve-volt batteries would drive the plane's electrics, but you needed two more to fire up the engines.

I was prepared to pay for the four batteries and to sacrifice the day to fetch them and cart them to the plane, although nothing of what Mills had to say – and there was plenty of that – was exactly calculated to inspire confidence.

In a moment of hubris I called Julia on the radio and told her about the Dakota. "But don't say anything about it for the time being. It may come to nothing. It may be a stupid idea."

I could hear from her voice that she wasn't exactly brimming with enthusiasm.

All the way to Jozini Mills explained in great detail what had originally been broken or rusted fast or missing and how he'd fixed or replaced it – all with what sounded to me like primitive, home-made spares.

"How did you get to hear about the plane?"

"In a bar in Margate. Retired nob of Military Intelligence. He told me the plane was one hundred per cent. But they had to clear out of the camp in the middle of the night after the Samora Machel mess. So then everything was left behind just like that. I didn't buy his story, but three years or so later I was near there; so I went to have a look. And there was the plane, overgrown with tambookie thorn and sickle grass."

"How long ago was that?"

"More than two years. I've been working on her for almost two years. Every time I have a few rand to spare I buy what I need, then I go and fit it."

"Was it from just standing there that she's in such bad repair? Two years of work is a lot on a plane that had nothing the matter with it – her."

"You should have seen her. Everything was the matter with her. I think they were stripping her or rebuilding her, I couldn't figure it out. But everything had been taken apart and a lot of the parts had gone missing. There was a big wooden box under the plane full of engine parts. With most of it I knew what went where; other bits I had to sit and reason out. I remember there was one thing in that box that I carried around with me for more than a year. I couldn't figure out where it went or what it did. I asked everyone who knew anything about Dakotas, but nobody knew. In the end I posted it to a guy who'd worked on Dakotas for years at Valhalla. So he let me know he'd never come across anything like that in a plane. Then he posted the thing back, but you know the post office. So there I was stuck without a part of the Dakota without knowing what I was stuck without. Don't know why I didn't ask Strydom, but of course you figure Strydom knows nothing about planes, so it would be a waste of time asking him. Then one morning I was at the dentist and I paged through *Farmer's Weekly*. And there was a photo of the selfsame bloody thing. And it was bugger-all of a Dakota. It was the foot valve of an old Climax windmill."

On the way back to Shabeni the mood started shifting slightly. His enthusiasm slowly but surely started yielding to uncertainty. He was thinking aloud what could still go wrong before he could get the plane up into the air.

"I don't know about the oil seals. You'll have to look-see once you have compression. They look OK. But you never know. Other things that can cause shit are the petrol pumps. Dunno. Maybe. And the magnetos and relays. And the wiring. I couldn't find an electroplan for the DC-3, and those wires had all been chomped up."

"Mice eat copper wiring?"

"Either that, or they'd carted it off. It had been chewed off everywhere. It hadn't been cut."

"So you were left guessing?"

"So I was left guessing, yes. What else? You try and you try till you start getting your bearings. I think I've figured her out. Time will tell. Only one of two things can happen: either everything works like a bomb, or she burns out."

"Why do you do this, Jock?"

"Why not? It's better than sitting around drinking, right?"

"Yes."

"Can I tell you something? If you want to be somebody special you have to do something special."

"You want to be somebody special."

"I want to be somebody, *ja*. Sure."

"What do you want to do with the Dakota when you've finished?"

"Fly. Even if it's just once."

Jock Mills was evidently someone whose confidence could take a knock very easily. He'd rather struggle along entirely on his own than be part of a team that didn't praise him constantly.

Strydom later recounted Jock's story about his short-lived career as a violinist. Apparently as a sixteen-year-old he was regarded as Pinetown's child prodigy – until he had to perform in front of an audience. Then everything went so disastrously wrong that at seventeen he gave away his violin. His explanation to Strydom was very simple. It had all been the audience's fault. "I was sure they would burst into applause the moment I started playing. They didn't. They just sat there. Unmoved. That threw me completely!"

He'd built up his Dakota in secret because he'd feared the same thing. He dreaded other people's scepticism and reams of reservations.

My cautious questions and concerned silences on the way to Jozini and back had been enough to make Mills doubt.

By the time we got back to the plane he'd got as far as admitting that he'd never before worked on such a plane, much less flown one.

"Everybody has a dream," he explained, in English. "You know what I mean. You start a thing like this, just for the hell of it. Just to try to prove something. If it doesn't work out – at least you've tried."

Apparently it wasn't only irritation and impatience that sometimes drove him to English. Uncertainty could also do it.

He'd be keeping his best English for later.

FIVE

I

With a huge effort we managed to wrestle two of the four batteries up the rungs of the ladder. The other two were connected in parallel from the ground as temporary boosters. It was high dusk already, but Mills would not hear of waiting. He wanted to get the plane's engines started. He wanted to know. He didn't want to lie awake all night wondering.

He'd hardly got the cables connected to the first battery, when he had to yank them off again. Somewhere there was the unmistakable smell of melting rubber and smoke.

"Short circuit somewhere. I think I know where." He disappeared into the baggage hold. Occasional snapping and hissing noises emanated from where he was investigating, and sparks and a few swear words and puffs of smoke. "Just as I thought," he said, returning with a broad grin. "The tail lights blew."

In due course all the batteries were connected and Mills installed himself in the cockpit.

"What are you going to do now?" I wanted to know, a bit more anxiously than I intended to betray. Because it was almost dark, and even in broad daylight I had no desire to share Jock Mills's maiden flight in his DC-3.

"Not to worry. We're not going to fly." He pressed a switch and suddenly two beams of light shot out over the thorn trees ahead of us.

"Shotto!" God's truth, the landing lights were actually working. "Now for the big moment." He was flicking switches up and down and pushing knobs in and pulling others out. Little dials flicked to and fro and every dial that showed willing was rewarded with an

83

audible response from Mills. It was a whole litany of "Ha!" and "Yes!" and "Whoa!" and "*Yebo!*" and "Absolutely fantastic!" with only here and there an isolated "Shit" or "Dammit" in between.

I went to stand next to him. "Should I get out, Jock?"

"No, why? We're not going to fly."

Suddenly there was this strange, asthmatic sound like when you're trying to crank an old car into life by hand. The left propeller miraculously started rotating fast once, twice, a few times. Then there was a bang. And dead silence.

"What was that?"

"Backfire. No problem."

Then again the same churning sound. This time it was the right propeller that started turning. But wonkily. Wobbly. Like a wagon wheel catching on a brake shoe. Then silence. Mills sat looking at his dials and pushed and pulled at some more switches.

"The good news is we have moved all twelve pistons."

"And the bad news?"

"Ignition."

"What about ignition?"

"Maybe. Dunno." He clearly had more pressing concerns on his mind than dealing with my anxious enquiries.

The left propeller started churning again. Once, twice, three, four times. Then without warning, like thunder on a sunny day, suddenly, magically, the engine took and roared!

Mills sat staring at me with something like disbelief and a bit of astonishment. Evidently he couldn't quite believe it himself. After a while he fed the engine slightly, and fed it more, and more and more – till the whole plane was vibrating with it. He couldn't get his fill of the racket. He sat with his head thrown back, his eyes shut tight as if listening with deep emotion to some incredibly delicate morsel of Mozart.

Then he killed the engine and started churning the right motor. A few times it was just about to take. And then it took and splut-tered and died. The third time it took properly, but the moment he fed it, the plane started shuddering and rattling as if it was landing in a donga field. I could see on Mills's face that this was bad news. He grabbed frantically at some switch, but the juddering was so bad that he missed it completely. When at last the engine died of its own accord, he remained sitting motionless for quite a while.

"And now?"

"Big shit."

"What?"

"Dunno. Mountings. Maybe. Maybe much bigger shit. Dunno." Our only light source was a five-cell torch and matches. The bakkie's lights were too low. I had to hold the torch while Mills checked the engine's mounting nuts one by one, tightened one or two, and in passing felt something here, tested something there, ran his fingers over everything, almost lovingly.

The engine wouldn't start again.

By ten o'clock the torch's batteries were flat and I had to strike matches till my fingers were burnt and blistered.

"Hell, Jock Mills, can't we just wait till tomorrow? What's driving you?"

"I must know what's wrong, otherwise I'll lie awake all night anyway."

"You've said yourself you're not going to fly tonight. We've almost run out of matches. Next thing we'll set the whole bangshoot alight."

"She's not a bangshoot."

"Whatever."

"I thought you were in a hurry. Or was all this bullshit about dying people just cheap talk or what?"

Quarter of an hour later we'd run out of matches as well. Mills carried on working in the dark.

I was slowly but surely getting the hang of Jock Mills. He took no account of time or place or rhyme or reason. If he was engrossed in something, the rest of the world vanished for him. There could have been some truth in Vukile's story that sometimes he'd work on the plane uninterruptedly for a week without eating and then be too weak to stay on his bike when he had to go back.

"Why don't I see a radio in this plane?" I asked after a while from the cockpit.

"Stolen."

"But there's no way you can fly without radio contact. How will you get permission to land?"

"One problem at a time, if you don't mind, Brand. Any case, if I have sixty dying people on board, I'd like to see who'll stop me when I'm trying to land."

"Sixty? Is there room for sixty?"

"Sixty Chopis, yes. Swahilis, whatever."

I walked off some distance and stood gazing at the night. Very far away on the plain a dog was barking incessantly. The Milky Way was a wind-blown cloud of light over the dark shoulder of the horizon.

I walked a long way across the landing strip almost to where it stopped, and listened to one cricket after the other piping down as I approached. There were little ant heaps everywhere and dead branches and even, in one spot, a largish aardvark burrow. There was a lot of rehabilitation to be done before any plane could take off from here.

I was on my way back when one engine suddenly started up again. Just like that. And a while later the second. I stood listening at a distance. Both engines were running smoothly. I could hear Mills gradually revving them up more and more until the drone modulated into a high, sweet, keening sound.

I walked faster.

The landing lights were switched on. The plane started moving. The two pale beams swept slowly across the flatcrown thorns and traced a wide circle until they were shining right on me. I walked towards the lights. With Mills you never could tell. He might just decide on the spur of the moment not to wait till tomorrow.

But the plane was brought to a halt. The lights were switched off. Then one engine. Then the other. The propellers kept turning for a while and then stopped. The silence of the night took over. The dog was still barking somewhere far, far away.

Joe Mills's Dakota was ready for take-off.

2

We made a bit of weak coffee with half a teaspoon of the instant stuff that had been in a sachet in Jock's shirt pocket, and meticulously divided three pieces of shop-bought rusks to dunk in our coffee. The roll-up mattress was too small for two and I curled myself up in one of the hollow canvas seats and fell asleep almost immediately.

The first birds woke me. Mills was outside greasing the wheel of a rusty wheelbarrow.

"What do you want to do with that?" I enquired.

"Cart petrol."

"In a wheelbarrow? Why not in the bakkie?"

Mills's grin was more embarrassment than relief. "I forgot about the bakkie. I'm so used to the Harley."

We went back the two hundred metres to where the army camp had been before and passed to the right of the row of toilets to a small concrete slab of about three metres by three with a steel cover in the centre. Mills lifted the cover. A cement staircase descended into the gloom. At the bottom there was a passage disappearing into the dark in both directions. The passage was about two metres wide and the floor, walls and roof were made of concrete girders. At first you could make out only two fifty-litre drums, but the longer you looked the more drums loomed up out of the darkness. Apparently in both directions there were two rows of drums packed all the way down the passage.

"Petrol?"

"All petrol. Two hundred and forty-two drums. Almost ten thousand litres. *Pasella* and for free."

"They've left it just like this for all these years?"

"I don't know what Military Intelligence's annual budget was. I suspect not even the President or the Minister of Defence really knew. But if they could afford to leave Dakotas lying around in the bush, this bit of petrol was peanuts to them."

We transported ten drums of petrol. That was the easy part. The plane's tanks were more than two metres above the ground. We parked the bakkie under the first tank, built a tower of empty drums on the back of the bakkie and lifted one full drum at a time onto the next level of the tower, until the tower was higher than the petrol tank. The process had to be repeated a few times, because the fuel gauges weren't operational, and we wanted to make sure that there was at least two hundred litres in each tank.

Mills used the rest of the morning to check everything one last time while I tried to fix the landing strip with a crowbar and a spade I'd picked up in the camp. It was a hopeless venture, getting it done in a few hours, because the runway was about a kilometre long and more than two hundred metres wide.

"Give me five hundred metres; that's more than enough," Mills assured me. "Five hundred by ten metres – right down the middle. And plant a stick or something at the end where the ant heaps start. A long stick with a cloth tied to it. Forget the rest."

That was a mistake.

And that was the last time that morning that he spoke Afrikaans.

At twelve o'clock he started with a few trial runs to test the flaps and tyres and the general performance of the bodywork, although he himself had to admit that eighty kilometres an hour on the ground could tell you nothing about what was going to happen up there.

"But at least if the wheels come off at a hundred Ks we know we have a problem. Metal fatigue will only start showing when it's too late to do anything about it." He wasn't trying to be funny. It was just one of the facts of the situation. The closer we came to zero hour, the more his fanatical side got the better of him. With so many unknowns in the equation, his chances of making a safe landing were fifty per cent at most. He was well aware of this, but after so many years of struggle and sweat he didn't want to sit and brood on that now. If his Dakota was ever going to fly again, it would have to be now or never.

After his sixth or seventh trial run Mills came to a stop, opened the door and beckoned me to get in.

"Never! I'm not going along!"

He indicated that he wanted to talk.

I dragged the ladder up and climbed in. The cockpit was awash with the smell of fuel.

"I'm gonna give her a go. She feels OK."

"Sure?"

"I'll give her a ten-minute workout and see how things develop."

"Good luck!"

"Take your bakkie to the end of the strip – just in case we don't get airborne."

I climbed down and stood watching Mills bolting the door from the inside and indicating through the side window that I should drive ahead. He looked completely calm, as if he were locking the back door before going to bed.

At the end of the landing strip, at right angles to it, was another one – slightly narrower and by the looks of it shorter, and I went and stopped around the corner to make sure that I was well out of the way.

Mills was on his way already.

When I switched off the bakkie, I could hear the high, almost hysterical keening of the engines close by me. I got out and saw the Dakota approaching. She was a hundred metres from me, far past the five hundred metres that Mills had talked of, and her wheels were barely half a metre above the ground. It looked as if she wasn't gaining height. The one wing was slightly lower than the other and there were fine rivulets of black fluid under both wings as if the propellers were leaking oil that was being smeared over the wings by the wind.

The plane cleared my head by a metre, about five metres from me, and just made it over the nearest thorn tree. It was only then that I noticed that the right wheel was dangling at an angle as if the axle was missing and the wheel had been tied to the wheel strut with a length of wire. Something was wrong, because although she was now visibly gaining altitude, she was veering – perhaps as a consequence of the lower left wing – more and more to the left.

I stood watching the Dakota slowly but surely climbing into the blue sky and eventually releasing itself from the semicircle and vanishing into the haze.

I couldn't get my hands to applaud, but in my heart I was applauding with both hands.

And I waited.

There was no longer a windsock. From which direction Mills would be approaching for the landing was thus impossible to predict. I drove back to the camp and sat waiting on the roof of the bakkie. Ten minutes. Twenty. Half an hour.

The wheel worried me. The drooping wing could still have been ascribed to Mills's inexperience in handling a Dakota, but the wheel was big trouble. He'd have to know his onions to land with only one wheel. And the big question was whether he had any idea about the wheel. Could a pilot see from the cockpit if a DC-3's one wheel had collapsed?

After an hour of waiting I was no longer concerned about the wheel. I was starting to wonder about the whole undertaking. It was just another instance of my tendency to ignore my common sense and to let myself be swept along by all sorts of dictatorial delusions.

There wasn't much to be done. I started tidying the tools.

At three o'clock that afternoon there was still nothing. Only the grey, hazy sky and the cicadas and the heat.

Long before four I accepted that I would not be seeing Jock Mills again. There was, by my calculations, not enough fuel in the tanks to stay aloft for such a long time.

But I kept waiting. Till long after dark.

There were plovers on the landing strip and crickets in the grass. Everything smelt of oil and petrol and dust. It felt to me as if a whole lifetime had spooled down in that single day.

The dog of the previous night was barking far away on the plain when at last I got into my bakkie to drive home.

3

Vusi was waiting for me. On the steps of the back stoep. Between two smoke-blackened lanterns.

"You're not dead?"

"No, Vusi. Why?"

Vusi decided to ignore the question.

"But if I don't have something to eat now, I'm not going to make it to sunrise."

"Did the bird fly?"

"Yes. He flew and didn't come back. I don't know what happened to him."

"Some birds do that."

There was freshly baked bread and dried beans and spaghetti, and although I'd eaten hardly anything for two days, I had to force the food down. My clothes were still reeking of petrol and every time I thought of the plane, I could see Jock Mills sitting with eyes tight shut listening to the singing engine. It was simply impossible to accept just like that that he was dead. There had to be another explanation. But what? The nearest other airport where a DC-3 could touch down safely was Durban. At a pinch Richards Bay. But why fly there in an unreliable plane that you'd liberated from the army if your plan had all along been to stay aloft for no more than fifteen minutes? None of the possible explanations that came to mind could reassure me.

Vusi came in and started making coffee.

"Didn't the radio call today, Vusi?"

"I did not hear."

"Have the people not come pestering around here again?"

"Lots. When they see the bakkie drive out, then they come. They took all your socks from the line."

"If that's the only damage, it's not a lot."

"We get lots of damage, *mnumzane*."

"Yes?"

"I find lots of snares. Yesterday's was nineteen."

"What!"

"Thursday was eleven. And the veld burned at Gezantombi."

"Hell, Vusi, is there anything left that can burn?"

"Down by the bulrushes. They wanted to drive out the rhebok."

"Those poor animals are so thin…"

"When are we going to the hospital?"

"Why?"

"I must get to Gwaja."

"Why?"

"I hear he's calling me."

"From who?"

"I hear him."

"You hear him calling you?"

"Yes."

I'd known him for long enough to realize that from Vusi you'd get only certain replies. He'd tolerate your questions up to a point and try dealing with them – and then shut up like a clam. And there was a reason for this. I'd often caught myself losing patience when I was trying to explain something to Vusi and he didn't catch on as fast as I might have wished. My way of protesting against Vusi's apparently slow uptake was to remain silent. Vusi understood nothing of a migratory bird's built-in electromagnetic compass or the fruit bat's echolocation. Vusi was no more patient with me when I couldn't understand how Gwaja could have called him without telephone or radio or messenger.

In time we learnt to respect each other's silences and impatience. Each learnt in his own way to understand when the other was venturing into a territory that he couldn't enter himself.

I sat in my outside room at night comparing data and listening to Vusi in his room talking in voices and murmuring incantations. I harboured the same cautious, tentative respect for it that Vusi accorded my strings of little figures. Each suspected that the other was in his own way a manipulator of arcane powers. If in every other respect we trusted each other completely, in this single respect we were cautious. I seldom went to bed at night before it was quiet in Vusi's room. For no particular reason. And Vusi never blew out his lantern before I'd locked the door of my outside room.

What questions Vusi nightly posed the great darkness about me and all my activities was difficult to guess. My questions, on the other hand, seemed self-evident to me: how many of Vusi's stories were pure superstition and fancy and how many of them were true?

His mother was an *igqira*, he often related, and she could cure people of illness. Not only illness of the body, also other illness that comes to torment the spirit. For Vusi, it seemed, there was no difference between the two – a sick spirit, he believed, made the body sick, and vice versa. If a small part of you was unwell, your whole being was sick.

He recounted once how from an early age he could see things happening that nobody spoke about. This led him to believe that either one wasn't supposed to talk about them, or that only he could see them. He and his mother. Because she did talk about these things. She told him when the ancestors emerged from their graves to confer with her; that sometimes she could see through walls and over mountains; that she could change her body to assume strange shapes; that she sometimes had the sensation of flying long distances to deliver messages. For her it was only a sensation; but Vusi actually saw her take off from her little grass mat and float out of the door and disappear.

These were strange stories that Vusi told very hesitantly – only a few times in all the years, and invariably late at night somewhere in the veld, with the moon down already, in that forlorn hour before the day starts breaking when the fluff-tail and the brown hyena call from the valleys.

With time this kind of story became scarcer, as the mistrust increased. Because I was a bad actor; I was dead curious and prepared to listen; I was eager to believe – but I just couldn't hide my sceptical nature well enough.

The fact was: Gwaja had called. There would no doubt be an opportunity some time or other to test Vusi's claim to telepathic powers.

I couldn't sleep. My mind kept dwelling on Jock Mills. Perhaps he was lying somewhere in the bush with broken legs or burn wounds or he was unconscious or dead. There was no point in going looking for him. There were hardly any roads in our area, and even if there had been, the undergrowth was so dense in many places that you could drive past twenty metres from an aeroplane wreck without seeing a thing.

I went to find the gas lamp and lit it, because my plan was to lie on my bed reading. It was no use. I just couldn't for the life of me concentrate and I suddenly discovered how dirty and dusty the room was.

As a rule I was out of the room by sunrise and returned only long after dark in the evenings. Usually by the feeble light of a candle or a lantern. Because the windows were so small and the edge of the thatched roof stuck out so far, you couldn't see very much inside even in broad daylight. The few times that we'd come across a snake in the house hadn't been because we'd seen it, but because it had foisted itself upon us. Some of them came and hibernated and left again without our being aware of them; the only evidence of their ever having been there was the desiccated strip of winter slough that they sometimes left behind between a bedpost and the wall. The gas lamp's hissing, uncongenial light was as a rule used only when absolutely necessary, and that night in that light I suddenly spotted months' worth of dust and dead flies and cobwebs and gecko skeletons that I hadn't been aware of before. We did now and then do some dusting and we swept the house fairly regularly, but with less and less enthusiasm as time went by. There was just too much dust wherever you went to have any hope of keeping the house clean. On the little patch of bare yard in front of the back stoep the dust puffed up around your feet, however slowly you walked. You breathed dust all day; you saw the sweat leaving brown mud tracks on your arms; in the afternoon under the shower the soap that you rinsed from your hair was a sticky brown gruel that trickled down your chest.

I extinguished the gas lamp and felt the darkness pressing down on me and went and sat on the front stoep.

Deep in the night, with the eyes of Jock Mills constantly before me, I inched my way step-by-step in the pitch-black darkness to the radio and tried to raise the clinic. Nobody would respond. I went looking for the matches and discovered that it was quarter past three. And then I slept. And dreamt Jock Mills was floating on a big white cloud with goggles on his eyes and waving at the little crowd of us on the ground – at me and Julia and Strydom and Vusi and Sister Roma and Vukile and Gwaja, and Gwaja hollering constantly at him through cupped hands to come down before it was too late.

At five o'clock Vukile at last responded.

He wanted to know about the Dakota. Apparently the whole station knew about the Dakota. Julia had promised she wouldn't talk until there were clear signs that the airlift plan had a chance of succeeding. But there was no changing dear Julia. About setbacks she could keep quiet for a very long time, but she couldn't keep anything to herself that could just turn out to be good news.

I decided to keep something to myself for a change. There was in any case no point in speculating about Jock Mills's unexplained disappearance.

"I haven't heard from him since yesterday, Vukile. I'll let you know as soon as I have news. I think he's... sorting out... a few problems. You know... technical things." I had yet to learn: if you have to lie, too little detail is far preferable to too much. "Wiring and stuff, you know. And mountings and... things."

"Julia wants to speak to you."

And suddenly she was there. Out of breath. As always.

"Brand?"

"Hello, Julia."

"I spoke to the Red Cross. They're going to try and help."

"How?"

"We have to let them know how many people there are and when we're bringing them. They're working with the army. I spoke to the army itself first, but they say we're in Mozambique, they only help South Africans."

"Same old story."

"But the Red Cross doesn't care. They say there's a whole tent town full of people somewhere already, I don't know where. Umbilo or somewhere."

I could feel my heart sinking into my boots. It was supposed to be good news, but without Jock Mills and his plane it was worth nothing to me.

"How are you two getting on?" Julia wanted to know. "Is that thing going to fly?"

"I don't know. I… don't know yet." Bloody Jock Mills. If he just hadn't buggered off into the air so pig-headedly and helter-skelter.

"How many people have you got there now?"

"It's getting more and more difficult to keep tally. A few over three hundred, I think. But thirty-four have died already and I think we're going to lose another few today. When will we see you?"

"I don't know. The weekend perhaps."

"Which weekend, Brand? It's Sunday today."

"Oh."

"Somebody will have to come and shoot us something again. If you come, bring Vusi along. Gwaja wants to see him."

Gwaja wants to see him.

Vusi knew it was Sunday, because that morning he emerged from his room in white pants and tackies and sat down in the shade next to the house darning clothes.

I went back to the Shabeni airstrip – against my better judgement, but driven by some blind hope. There was no sign of the Dakota. There was just this little bit of stupid wind blowing across the plateau and driving dust and tumbleweed and dislodged clumps of grass across the bare veld.

I had no real choice: I'd have to go and tell the people at the mission station. They'd have to devise another plan. Mills with his Dakota was no longer an option. Apart from which I'd have to notify the police and civil aviation.

I went to pick up Vusi.

If the station a week before had seemed rather agitated and somewhat pillaged, that was nothing compared with the conditions now prevailing there. It was now a squatter camp. There were easily twice as many people as the previous week. Of the wind blowing up on the plain, there was not a sign here. A thick pall of smoke hung over the hospital. And a stench that is difficult to describe. Somebody was shovelling spatters of vomit and diarrhoea and other human waste of an indeterminate nature into a bucket. But it was more than just that. The air was sticky with a smell of urine and putrefaction hanging everywhere between the shelters. At the far end of what had been the banana avenue, against a bank that had previously shown remains of kikuyu, two people were skinning a dog, I hope dead, with a penknife, the skeleton just about visible under the sparse hair. Next to them a woman was lying on her side with her hands under her face; she just now and again averted her face slightly in an attempt to drive away the flies; her gaze was fixed on the skinning.

Vukile was the first to come out. Somebody who didn't know him would have thought he was in some state of anaesthesia. "Yes, brother." He came and put his hands on my shoulders and did the same with Vusi. "I hope you've brought us another hippo." His odd little laugh put in a sudden appearance, but very wearily.

On our way to the front door Julia came running round the corner with a child in her arms. "Vukile, come and help!" she called as she went in by the front door.

"How's the Dakota coming on?" He'd evidently forgotten that he'd asked me the same question that morning.

"It's taking time."

There were in the region of forty people around my bakkie. They were pushing each other aside in an attempt to see if the bakkie had brought food. A woman with a child on her hip came and stood next to me. The child was sucking at one of her stretched, thin breasts. She was making soft mewling noises all the time, as if crying, but there were no tears in her eyes.

"This looks bad," was my spontaneous reaction.

"It's worse." Vukile was following Julia. "Take a stroll and look for yourself."

Gwaja must have seen the bakkie because he came hurrying up and greeted Vusi profusely by hand. He was a gigantic man with long arms and a way of talking with exaggerated gesticulations. Whatever urgent matter they had to discuss with each other would by custom only be discussed later. Vusi was always very particular that one left the most important news for last.

I tried to walk through the terrain, but turned back halfway. My legs were starting to feel unsteady under me. I got the feeling that I wasn't really there, I was floating, I was dreaming. There was no barbed wire and there were no heaps of corpses, but I felt part of a jerky, washed-out, silent black-and-white movie of Dachau. Everyone was sitting or lying in dead silence – on the bare earth, a few on grass mats or blankets – and everybody stared at me, motionless, curious, expectant, as if I'd been some alien creature who could, just possibly could, with a word or a gesture, call down quails and manna from the skies.

In the first minute it was the smell that got to me. But after a while the eyes started taking over. There were eyes wherever I looked. Pair upon pair of dull, staring, expectant eyes. I could read death everywhere, and that was bad enough. I could see the shattered, last bit of light in the eyes, dark light, as in very old mirrors full of stains and surface cracks – but in the last shred of light left in each pair of eyes there was hope. Obdurate, obstinate, unabashed hope.

I tried talking to some of them. First Swazi. "*Kuyini ligama lakho?*" Later English. "Where do you come from?" They just sat staring at me. "What is your name?" Now and again one nodded or shook his head, but I could see they did not understand me. They accepted that I was the bearer of good tidings, I was bringing deliverance, I'd come to make the difference; they would wait.

The stench I could get used to. The dry snot and blowflies and slobbery splatters of tummy-run I could try not to see. But the hope was something terrible.

The church was open. Everywhere on the benches people were lying asleep. For the first time in the seven years that I'd known Mbabala, there were no candles burning in front of the altar. It was always dark in the church, because the shutters were closed. I went to sit on one of the front benches and closed my eyes. I could feel my innards constantly blocking my throat from below. A woman got up from her bench and came and knelt next to me. She tried to say something to me. All of them were all the time trying to talk to us and none of us could understand anything. I could hear she was repeating the same sentence over and over, pleading, almost desperate.

As it was, the situation was bad enough, with so many mouths to feed. But that almost none of us could speak their language just made one feel so much more hopeless. Of all of us Gwaja and Sister Roma were the only ones who could understand Shangaan, but according to them the people spoke a dialect of Shangaan that was very difficult to follow. A few could apparently speak a form of Portuguese, but not one of us could understand a scrap of it. The woman took my hands and held them tightly and kept on saying the same thing. We'd shared a continent side by side for a lifetime, she and I, but we were like beings from different planets trying to transmit a vital message to each other and not succeeding.

Then, suddenly, I clicked that it was an English word she was saying. "Please!"

"Please?"

She started nodding vehemently. "Please! Please!"

She was wearing a torn dress that must have been a floral dress once, there was a wooden comb in her hair and she wore a few strings of red beads tightly around her throat. This made her exceptional, because the rest of them had hardly any clothes and no embellishments whatsoever. She'd probably formerly been some induna's wife.

I don't know where Julia came from. She was on her knees in front of the altar. She seemed to be praying.

Previously, in the time when Father Holm officiated and Sister Roma and company were still very set on the daily prayer sessions, I often on a Sunday attended the morning service just after daybreak with Julia and then admired her for the almost fierce devotion, the total surrender with which she participated in every moment of it. But the longer I witnessed this the more my admiration turned to amazement. Especially after she told me about Sister Superior Mary Lambert. Because in a way the sister superior was no more than a replica of P.W. Botha and Ulrich Neumann and Tielman Krige. After them and everything that they represented, she had unequivocally and irrevocably turned her back on them – why not also on the Church?

She told me only once about her father, and only once about Neumann – although she often referred to him; she told me about P.W. only once (often about the National Party, but only once about P.W.); she often referred to her stepmother Augusta, but only once told me the story of her and Augusta. And every one of these people left an indelible scar on her. About Mary Lambert she told me again and again. Each time in greater detail. As if with the telling and all the retelling she was trying to form a scab over the lesion Mary Lambert had left.

She was eighteen when she was inducted into the convent. Twelve years at school and a year at the Potchefstroom University for Christian Higher Education had not once imperilled her virginity and her innocence. Although she would later reflect with some bitterness on all the false manifestations of spotlessness, the convent placed the seal on an unblemished youth.

The thick walls and high windows made her feel safe. The black dress and bib and soutane, the prayer beads and icons, she believed, were the clearest possible way of repudiating Tielman

Krige and the National Party and Augusta and the Three Sister Churches' judgemental pulpit cloths and P.W. Botha's admonitory white finger.

Mary Lambert took her under her wing and prayed with her and dried her tears. Mary the sister superior spent many days embroidering with her in the garden until they were overtaken by dusk, and taught her about the incomprehensible divine love that comprehends everything and covers everything and forgives everything. Everybody knew that she was the sister superior's pet. And she didn't mind, because it was pleasant to be somebody's pet for the first time in her life. That whole first winter she went to put a hot-water bottle in the sister superior's bed every evening and in the first summer brought her frangipani flowers in a saucer every morning. It was an indescribably wonderful experience to be so surrounded by the tender love of God and the unselfish love of all about her. In the afternoon, when she was on her own, she climbed the fig tree in the courtyard and on one of the highest branches she'd lie and send up prayers of thanksgiving for her deliverance from a world in which she'd never really felt at home.

At the end of Julia's third winter in the convent the sister superior fell ill. Everyone took turns to keep vigil by her. From eight to twelve at night was Julia's shift. But the others overslept more and more often and Sister Superior Mary never wanted her to go and wake them. Later she was managing the whole vigil by herself, and sometimes fell asleep on the little cot next to the sister superior's. Where she awoke one morning just before daybreak to find Sister Superior Mary Lambert lying behind her back without a stitch of clothing, caressing her breasts and kissing her in the neck with a warm and open and writhing mouth.

Every time that I saw the abandon with which Julia prayed, like that afternoon in the dark little church, her head half at an angle against the clay-and-mortar wall, I remembered Mary Lambert. The one time I'd asked her whether Mary Lambert had done anything to her relationship with the Church, she'd shaken her head indignantly. "But P.W. Botha…"

"P.W. Botha *was* the National Party. The sister superior was not the Church. The National Party taught me that white Afrikaners were the chosen people; the Church taught me that all people are sinful."

Julia hadn't seen me. She was on her way out of the church. I put out my hand to her and she took it and came to sit next to me. "What are you doing here?"

"I don't know. I was walking about outside and…"

"And then it got to you."

"I don't know how you stand it."

She gripped my arm with both her hands and pressed her cheek against my shoulder for a moment. "It's bad, Brand, I know. But you get used to it. Not actually used. You shrug it off. You'll see. You… must."

"You must?"

"What else?"

"I guess that's a good reason."

"Come and see."

We went outside. The light was suddenly blindingly white on the walls. I could hear the woman with the beads calling after us.

A little bare-bummed boy was approaching us. He must have been about six and there was little more than kneecaps to him. He held out a handful of coloured feathers to Julia. "Ah, thank you! More feathers! Thank you very much." The child's smile revealed two rows of little half-rotten teeth. "Since the first day I fed him, he's forever bringing me things. Feathers and stones and porcupine quills. He's my little sparrow boy." Julia picked him up and carried him along on her hip.

"I want to go and show you something." She was making her way through the branch shelters to a dark rim of trees around the mission station. "We're all helping. Even Vukile. And the new people who arrive with a little bit of reserve strength are a great help. And Gwaja… you should see Gwaja. In the evenings till after dark."

"What are you talking about?"

"The landing strip. We're more than halfway."

Through the narrow strip of trees I could see the clearing. Wordlessly I followed her to the other side of the trees. In front of me, on the stretch of level ground to the south of the mission station, the veld had been cleared of guarri and stamperwood and feverberry and raisin bush. Thirty metres wide, half a kilometre long.

An airstrip for Jock Mills's DC-3.

SIX

I

A few things went wrong simultaneously the next day. And as tends to happen, all these things in the end claimed their due in unison: consequences started to turn into causes. By dusk the inventory went more or less like this: we had to cut the throat of a rhebok that had been caught in a snare barely five hundred metres from the house; our only borehole started spluttering; I had my first altercation with Vusi in more than a year; and there was no news of Jock Mills.

In retrospect, the great silence surrounding Mills was the worst news, because the borehole was, after a few days' rest, almost back to its normal strength, but that morning the borehole was out-and-out disaster number one. The hole had, according to Strydom, been sunk by prospectors some years ago, and instead of finding whatever it was they were looking for, they'd found water. It was the borehole that had determined us to build there. For five years we could rely on having a few hundred litres a day. A smallish solar panel sufficed, providing us with enough water to shower and wash dishes. Without that we would have been lost. In the beginning, before the borehole was fully equipped, we would cart big drums of water from the Bápe and pump it into the tank by hand. But the Bápe was now dry. We'd have to cart water from the mine or the mission station, and both were over fifty kilometres away.

The argument with Vusi was a stupid business. I wanted to know why Gwaja had called him. And Vusi ignored the question. Initially I could tell myself that if it hadn't been for the borehole and the rhebok, I wouldn't have taken exception to Vusi's sullen silence.

Later I had to admit that I'd been fed up for a long time with that blank silence that could sometimes follow an innocent question.

It was just after we'd been to cut the rhebok free of the snare. Vusi had heard the scuffling against the hillside behind the house and gone to investigate and come across the buck with its left front paw caught in a wire. The animal was three-quarters dead and I had to cut its jugular.

That put both of us on a wrong footing. Then, at dusk while Vusi was making the fire, I asked about Gwaja. And one word led to the next. The little bit of water in the kettle was red-brown, as if there were only mud left in the borehole, and that didn't really help to cheer up the two of us. Then it started with Vusi's silence. And it was further messed up by my saying I was tired of his crotchety moods.

Vusi was packing coal into the stove. He put the pail down, leaving the stove plate just like that to one side, and went outside without lighting the fire. It was only when he heard I was following him that he stopped and turned round.

"Talk to me, Vusi. Don't just stand there."

"White people don't understand those things."

"How are we ever going to understand if nobody wants to tell us about it?"

"You don't want to hear, you want to see. You don't believe if you don't see."

"Nonsense, Vusi. I know lots of things happen of which we understand nothing – but they happen, even if we don't know how."

"Like what do you believe that you don't understand?"

"Like that the weavers know in September already whether it's going to be a wet or a dry year. And—"

"That's because you see it with your eyes, otherwise you wouldn't have believed that either."

"That's what I do all day, trying to help find out how some things work that we don't understand."

"Your kind of things. You laugh at my things, *mnumzane*."

"No, Vusi!"

"I see when you laugh inside your head."

"Like at what?"

"The big snake with the lantern. The dead people who talk. My mother who turned into a baboon. I'm not talking to you any more about Gwaja." He was walking away from me.

"I thought you were going to make a fire, Vusi!" He pretended to be deaf and carried on walking.

"Vusi, come here, I'm talking to you, dammit!"

"It will burn."

Vusi's voice betrayed everything that he'd tried to hide by walking away: indignation and impatience and irritation.

I went into the kitchen and took the box of matches from the shelf next to the stove. Exactly where he'd put it that morning before daybreak in the candlestick after lighting the candle. I was on the point of striking a match when I saw the smoke: a thin spiral curling up out of the coal. Then I opened the grid. The paper wasn't burning. The kindling on the paper wasn't burning. Only the coal was smouldering. I stood watching a little bluish flame climbing from among the coal and cautiously licking up into the air – small, and then bigger and bigger, as if the layer of air above the coals was catching fire. Then, suddenly, the whole mouth of the grid was full of flame.

I looked into the mouth again. The newspaper and kindling had still not caught. I sat on my haunches and watched the flames burning from the top down.

Vusi's bedroom door was open and a lantern was burning on the table, but he wasn't there. He was nowhere around the house.

I boiled water and washed my hands and face and ate, my ears pricked up all the time listening for Vusi's return. It had been a long day. I'd been at Jozini at half-past six that morning to report Mills's disappearance. But before going to the police station, I'd first tried to phone the aerodromes at Richards Bay and Pietermaritzburg and the airport at Durban from a phone booth. The two aerodromes knew nothing about an unscheduled Dakota, and the switchboard at Durban airport repeatedly kept me waiting until I was cut off, or switched me through to someone else who never replied. At the police station, later, the man behind the counter, a warrant officer whose name I forgot on the spot, was clearly not very interested. It took a lot a sweet-talking to get him to take a statement. He felt that a pilot who took off in his plane was not necessarily missing because he hadn't returned within a day or two to the same aerodrome. After a long exposition of the circumstances he at one stage seriously started considering investigating a case of theft of an army aeroplane. The most I could wring from him in the end was an undertaking to inform civil aviation of the unscheduled flight of a Dakota without radio communication.

On my way back I couldn't shake off the thought that I'd just stabbed Jock Mills in the back, albeit posthumously.

That evening while waiting for Vusi on the back stoep, there was constant lightning far in the south, the first time in a very long while. And that was the first good thing that had happened to me all day.

Vusi turned up only after nine. He was aloof and sullen. He didn't want to eat. He went into the kitchen and put more coal into the stove and boiled himself some water. We didn't mention the fire at all.

I went and latched the front door and made sure that the screens on all the windows were closed. When I went to fetch a candle to take to the room, Vusi came in by the back door and put the kettle down on the stove. For a moment we were both a mite unsure; we stood wordlessly and a bit vulnerably opposite each other without looking at each other. Then, on his way out, Vusi said: "Gwaja says the bird didn't fall."

"What?"

Vusi went into his room and was closing the door, but I was too fast for him. I quickly put my hand on the lower half of the door. "I'm sorry, Vusi, I didn't hear properly." I had in fact heard, but I was afraid I might have misheard. "What did you say?"

"The big bird didn't fall."

My mouth was open, ready to ask "How do you know?" but I bethought myself. And nodded. And removed my hand from the door.

Vusi closed the door and slipped the bolt.

2

In one respect Vusi and Strydom were very similar. Their communications were small and often inconspicuous islands in a great ocean of silence – islands so far removed from one another that it didn't always occur to you to link them.

Afterwards, when everything was over, it was easier to spot certain things that in the heat of the moment had escaped everybody's attention. Later it was self-evident that Strydom in his own unique and roundabout way had been looking for the origin of man, possibly because he wished to deduce something from that for himself about the final fate of humanity. Vusi was in conversation with his most distant ancestors because he wanted to know about next year's rain and the leopard in tomorrow's footpath. For both of them it was a very personal, secret investigation about which they were very rarely prepared to talk.

I started remembering some of the half sentences, the incidental comments, the few anecdotes that Vusi had entrusted to me here and there over the years. Two other people who had spent so long more or less constantly in each other's company would probably with time have had fewer secrets from each other, but our knowledge of each other did not come easily. And for that there were many reasons. Vusi's Afrikaans was even more limited than my stunted and stilted Zulu and that in itself was enough reason to put a damper on a natural exchange of thoughts. But in addition we were both still victims of the society in which we'd grown up and in which black people and white people had to coexist on either side of an invisible wall, like fish in the same pond but separated by glass. It went much deeper than a language problem or a superficial prejudice – it was a blind assumption that the other one thought, felt, experienced things in a different way, *was* different.

That afternoon next to the Bápe while we were waiting for the baboon troop, I had indeed laughed when Vusi told me that his mother could change herself into a baboon in plain sight and that she could fly. And yes, I *had* laughed about the story of the great water snake that sometimes just before dark emerges from the river with a lantern on its head – and about the messages that the ancestors transmitted so regularly to those who knew how to listen. I had laughed. And it was too late to explain now that I hadn't laughed because I wanted to belittle something. I was indeed sceptical, about some things much more than others, but I had enough respect for the paranormal not just to dismiss anything out of hand as hogwash.

It was a long route from *Homo erectus* to *Homo sapiens*. I've always believed that there is still a long road ahead. We are gazing into a grey haze surrounding us, in which we sometimes, just sometimes, in a fraction of a second almost recognize something. Perhaps we are on the way towards *Homo intuitivus*.

That's why I believed that Vusi had lit the fire by some means other than matches – and accepted Gwaja's word that the Dakota had landed safely. But every time, an hour later, I was much less sure. I wanted to talk my suspicion away and give them the benefit of the doubt, but for Vusi that was not good enough.

It was my doubt as well as my will to believe that drove me to Mbabala the next day.

Every time I got there, there were noticeably more people. I became aware that I was trying to look past them. I could see them and I even greeted some of them, but I tried not to notice the emaciated faces.

Vukile was sitting behind his desk swatting flies, for no apparent reason ignoring the blowfly circling his head. He was a weary man and by the looks of it a bit confused, like somebody who'd just discovered that he was on the wrong train.

"I'll send for Julia."

"No, don't. We must talk."

"Still no Dakota?"

"Not yet. I think we may have lost it."

"Please, God!" He put down the fly-swatter. "How?"

"I'm not sure yet. I'll have to make a few phone calls."

"Go ahead. Where's Mills?"

"That is part of the problem. He went on a fifteen-minute test flight the day before yesterday… and didn't come back."

"Oh shit, man!"

"Maybe Durban Airport can help us."

The raggle-taggle telephone directory, a good five years old, was suspended on an impala thong from the bookshelf behind Vukile.

"I'll look up the number."

"I've got it. How's Julia?"

"Brother, she's a star. But it's getting to her. We are losing more and more people every day. We're out of medicine. And more or less out of food as well."

"May I?" My hand was on the telephone.

"Sure."

Almost an hour's worth of hassle later it was established beyond doubt that the Dakota hadn't arrived in Durban. Civil aviation confirmed that they'd been notified of the missing plane, but that all their enquiries had come to nothing. All planes in the vicinity had been asked to be on the alert for a wreck, but nothing had turned up.

Jock Mills's DC-3 had disappeared into thin air.

How the news reached Julia was not very clear later and probably not of much importance anyway. Somebody said she was sleeping, because she'd worked through the previous night, so I didn't go looking for her. But by nine o'clock, while I was sterilizing hypodermic needles for Vukile, Sister Roma came to suggest that I should perhaps look in on Julia – things weren't well with her.

Vukile was with her. She was lying on her bed crying, surrounded by small, fluffy guinea-fowl feathers that the child must have brought her again.

"I gather somebody told her about Mills."

I sat down next to her and took her hand. "Julia? What's the matter?"

"She doesn't talk. I've been trying to give her an injection, but she refuses."

"Julia? Talk to me."

She lay motionless looking at the ceiling, her arms on either side of her body. She made not a single sound, but her mouth was slightly distorted as if she was crying, and tears were running down her temples.

"Julia, just say something, please."

"You're just tired, Julia, that's all. What you need is a few hours' sleep. Please let me give you an injection. It will help you relax." She seemed to hear nothing at all.

Vukile glanced at me sideways and we nodded in unison. The next moment the syringe was in Vukile's hand and I had to jump to pin Julia's arms to the bed. But it wasn't that simple. She started thrashing with her legs, suddenly enraged and wild, but still without making a sound. Vukile tried to ward her off with one arm, but the next moment her foot struck him against the shoulder, sending the syringe arcing through the air. Gwaja suddenly appeared from nowhere and it took the three of us to get her under control so that Vukile could inject her. She calmed down almost immediately and a few minutes later she was asleep.

Only then did I notice the sparrow child hiding crouched down in the corner. I picked him up and felt that he was trembling from head to foot. He was scared to death and I could see he was clenching something in each fist. I cupped my free hand in front of him. One fist placed a little black pebble carefully into my hand and the other a blood-red loerie feather.

Vukile was not impressed. "We better take him outside. He's become a real nuisance." But his attention was immediately redirected to Julia. He was taking her pulse. "She'll sleep for at least three hours."

"OK. Let's go."

"Same thing happened to Sister Roma day before yesterday," Vukile said as we went out. "I suppose I'm next in line."

We were outside by the time I realized that Gwaja was not with us; he'd stayed behind.

He was on his knees next to her bed when I reached them, swinging a small forked stick slowly to and fro above her head.

"Why are you doing that?" I asked. With Gwaja I always had to speak Zulu, because his only knowledge of Afrikaans and English was a "Thank you" here and a "Yes" there.

Gwaja signalled to me not to talk.

Only later, outside, while he was washing his hands in a bowl and the forked stick as well, he answered my question. "She's walking alone in the darkness. A woman doesn't walk alone like that."

"And what does the forked stick do?"

"The forked stick does nothing. It's a matumi stick. The voice of the big river is talking to her. When you're tired and you're lying next to a river with lots of water, then you sleep the sleep of two people in one night."

"Thank you, Gwaja."

"I must go and help in the kitchen."

"Before you go and help, Gwaja. Just tell me. Where is the big bird that didn't fall?"

He looked up and smiled – as one smiles at a stranger behind enemy lines who has just identified himself as a comrade – and shook his head. "I don't know. But he's sitting and waiting. He's waiting to fly again."

3

Julia slept soundly till long after midnight, without stirring. And then woke up a few times, and asked for water, and talked to me incoherently, and slept again. An hour. And again two or three hours. And then till after dawn. All the time I was close to her. I lit a candle and placed it next to her and sat holding her hand.

Went to sit in the kitchen and tried to read a book. Looked for something to eat. Went to stand on the little front stoep listening to the voices outside in the dark, turtle doves, a guinea fowl down near the river, laughing children. That is the one thing that I will remember for ever after – those children were always laughing. At three o'clock in the morning you'd wake up and hear a child laughing somewhere. They complained when they were hungry, and cried when they were in pain, but the rest of the time they laughed. As on the night before there was constant lightning very far to the south, a continuous play of light somewhere beyond the invisible flank of the horizon. But by now I knew better than to build my hopes on that. I went back into the house and lit a second candle and stayed with Julia. I wanted to be close enough to her to see when she stirred, if she should ask for something.

Candlelight does things to one's face. It shows up more of everything. It makes beautiful eyes look more beautiful; it makes a tired mouth seem more tired. A thin hand seems thinner. An uncertain smile seems just that little bit more uncertain. I had an opportunity, that night, to look a bit more attentively at everything, at myself too, but especially at Julia, and by candlelight to see what I hadn't seen for a long time – and to see quite a lot that had changed in the meantime.

She had indeed aged. And that was understandable. The previous month had posed physical and emotional challenges that few people could have survived. But something in her face had got softer, as if she was now prepared to live with certain things that she hadn't felt up to previously. It was a tired, worn-out face that by candlelight seemed softer and more vulnerable, more innocent.

I remembered again with how much rancour she used to refer to Augusta, her stepmother, who never wanted her to call her Ma. She was six years old when the woman that she'd known as her mother, suddenly one morning, in between corn flakes and yoghurt, announced:

"It's time that you knew, Julia. I'm not your mother. Your mother died when you were just a baby. You can call me by my name, I don't mind. Call me Augusta." Augusta was nobody's mother. The closest she could get to being anything other than Augusta was when she could be someone else in an official capacity. The wife of the local MP, Mrs Krige. Chair of the reading group. Treasurer of the WAU. Dedicated scheduler of her husband's daughter's preparedness training – Mondays squash, Tuesdays first aid and SCA, Wednesdays ballroom, Thursdays debating society, Fridays Voortrekkers, autumn holidays NP youth camp, winter holidays Voortrekker camp, spring holidays survival camp. Her father was in the Cape for six months of the year and for the other six months too busy to be at home. He was serving the nation. "My father didn't know what to do with a daughter, so he left me with Augusta," she said one day. "Augusta never wanted a child, not even a stepchild, so she scheduled me. You'll just have to forgive me if I don't always know how to handle affection."

Once when she woke up, I asked whether she wasn't hungry. She nodded and turned on her side and kept sleeping. Just as well, because there were no longer bunches of half-green bananas and almost-ripe papayas on the little dining-room table. In fact there was almost nothing to eat. A tin of sardines, a bit of tomato sauce, a packet of pasta, half a bag of rusks. I ate some of the rusks.

There was hardly any moon and after midnight the branch screens behind the hospital were almost totally quiet. Here and there you could see the remains of what had in the early evening been fires to heat water – a scrap of light as comfort against the dark, but by this time only a few embers with a greyish glow. The air was motionless and sticky, heavy with woodsmoke and the saltpetre of urine and sweat.

It had been a totally different place when I first got to know it, before the departure of Father Mundt. In the days when it still rained. Often over a weekend I went to play chess with the priest and listen to music – always Corelli and Haydn and Vivaldi. We'd play until late at night, in summer often with continuous rain on the roof, and at eleven drink a last little glass of port outside on the stoep, with the sky full of heavy clouds and endless streaks of lightning in the south, the earth warm and soaked and steaming under the green lawns, and listen to the exuberant calling of wild geese and plovers beyond the dark wall of wild banana next to the clinic.

It was still like that in the first year after Julia's arrival. That first week in November, a few weeks after we'd met, Father Holm, who at that time had been at the station for a while, summoned me. "Take the child into the veld for a bit," he said, "I can see the loneliness is getting to her. I don't think she realized how far in the bundu we're stationed. Her eyes seem reddish with weeping in the morning." I took her across the river to the Bápe and into the stretch of forest with its multicoloured millipedes and black moths and Spanish moss and brushwood; deep into the dark tunnels where the brown mushrooms grew in the mouldered remains of age-old matumi stumps, and out at the other side, up the steep banks and high up against the sheer rock faces above the Bápe's Baboon Kloof.

I gazed at her mouth all day. Her lips were always moist. And there was a darkness in the brown of her eyes like the dark glow of the rock slabs next to the Bápe when it drizzled for days on end. It upset me to realize that I was seeing the bush almost for the first time. I was experiencing everything around me through her senses. I smelt the compost under the trees, heard the loeries in the damp canopy above, I laughed and sweated and breathed and walked like someone who had never done it before. And something kept telling me that she knew it.

At dusk, while we were waiting in the branches of a strangler fig for the troop to return to their sleeping quarters, I noticed that she was sitting with her eyes closed all the time. "Are you tired?" I asked.

"No."

"Why are you closing your eyes?"

"I'm praying."

"You're praying?"

"Don't you ever pray?"

"Not as a rule when I'm sitting in a tree."

"In the convent there was a big fig tree in the courtyard with these high branches. I often climbed into the tree at night, then I straddled the highest branch and prayed. In summer I could always feel the tree swaying under me when the wind blew, then I felt part of the tree and as if the tree was praying with me."

"You were in a convent?"

"Three years."

"You were a nun?"

"Yes."

"Why?"

"Why not?"

The first baboons appeared on the rock face opposite us and we didn't talk about it again that day. But later she would admit more than once that her years in the convent, like her training as a nurse and her days of wandering in Europe and that confused half-year in politics, were only part of her way of repeatedly saying no to a system of which she was an unwilling part, which she could not escape, which she wanted to resist.

She had been liberated, eventually, yes; she could fulfil her need to stand by the poor, to guide the lost, to care for the hungry – but ultimately her rebellion was not against hidebound parents and cunning sisters superior and corrupt politicians: it was against the earth itself. And that had broken her spirit that night, it was to be hoped only temporarily. All the previous times there had been a person, people, a committee, a cabinet, a face, somebody with a name – Mary Lambert, Jan Tolmay, Tielman Krige and his wife Augusta (née Strauss), P.W. Botha, name all the names – against whom she could lie fulminating through many a night. But suddenly, now, there was no one. No face. An absence. A great, almighty, inexplicable, empty Nothing. Nowhere a cloud; no wind; no footprint or fingerprint; no sign of rain or any manifestation of mercy; no hope. An endless, desolate landscape full of skeletons and motionless tumbleweed and dead ant heaps.

She woke up just after dawn and smiled when she saw me standing next to her bed. "I dreamt it was raining."

"It must have rained somewhere. There was lightning all night."

"Probably over the sea. It only rains over the sea."

Vukile knocked at the back door and came in straight away.

"No more injections for me, thank you!"

"OK. Provided you stay in bed."

"I can't."

"You must. Otherwise… pssst!" With thumb and forefingers he pressed an imaginary hypodermic needle to her arm. "Brother, I have a message for you. Guy called Jimmy phoned. Jimmy or Johnny or Jamie or something. Says you must wait for him at your place this morning."

"Why? Who? What for?"

"Line was bad. Between ten and eleven today. Something about a motorbike."

"A motorbike? What motorbike?"

Apparently the line had been so bad that Vukile wasn't even sure whether it had been a man or a woman. It had sounded like a woman, but the Jimmy or Johnny made him think it was a man. And he wasn't sure whether it would be that morning or the following morning.

Jock Mills's motorbike was still parked in my yard. But only Vusi and I knew that. Whoever Johnny or Jimmy was, he couldn't be referring to Mills's bike – except if he was on his way to collect the bike at Shabeni.

When I got home just before nine, there was a battered red Volkswagen Beetle parked up next to the outside room. Vusi was at hand immediately. "Here's a man looking for you. I don't know him."

"Where is he?"

"He's walking around here."

The man came round the corner of the house. Slightly built, denim trousers and shirt, broad-rimmed felt hat on his head.

We walked towards each other. And something about his walk bothered me. It wasn't a man's way of walking.

"Mr Brand?" It wasn't a man's voice either.

"Jimmy?"

"Jenny Grobler. You got my message?"

"About a motorbike?"

"Yes. Morning." The hand and handshake were those of a woman. There were bracelets of copper and beads and ivory on both her wrists. Her skin was dark and I got the impression it wasn't from the sun. She took off her hat and a shock of black hair spread itself over her face in slow motion. "I see it's standing here."

"You're talking about Jock Mills's bike?"

"Yes."

"What do you know about Jock?"

"He sent me to fetch his bike."

"Sent?"

"Yes."

"Where is he?"

Jenny Grobler checked her watch. A man's watch. "He's landing in two hours' time on a landing strip somewhere around here that you know about. I hope."

"With that Dakota?"

"That was the plan, yes."

I was working myself into a blind rage. At Jock Mills. And at the same time I was trying to get behind what was happening in front of me. This man who was a woman all of a sudden and the damned Mills that I'd time and again seen in my mind's eye burning to death in a rusty DC-3 in a desolate patch of sickle bush and who now suddenly had nothing the matter with him – all of that and the pretty pearls of sweat over this Jenny's mouth: it was all just a bit too much too soon for me.

"…Oh." From nowhere Vusi was suddenly by our side as well. "So… the plane didn't fall?"

"I'm sorry?"

"Where is he taking off from?"

"Manzini."

"Swaziland?"

She just raised her eyebrows slightly.

"Do you know him?"

Her eyebrows lifted further. "Jock?"

"The bugger!"

She appraised me for a moment as if anew, replaced her hat on her head and checked her watch again. "Are we going in your car or mine?"

4

There was Esta. And then there was a little bit of Dirkie. And then Kristi. And then there was Julia. But Julia was different, because she was more than just an episode. I understood Julia less than all the others and railed against her the most of all; I desired her and resisted her. I loved her. Kristi too, I suppose, but that had possibly been more a matter of emotional insecurity than love. (That's not true, I know. But about such things you never know for sure.)

Kristi and I were close friends for I suppose about five years. We studied together and on the weekends went together to do plant surveys in the Magaliesberg and we cycled and learnt to hang-glide, and even on several occasions produced somebody that the one thought would be a good match for the other. We were too used to each other to be aware of each other. Later I could never remember when that started changing. We were sharing a house with four other students and I noticed that I was inclined to get irritated when she came home too late at night; I started phoning her when she went to visit family over weekends; I "forgot" to pass on telephone messages from other men. Some or other dusk of some or other autumnal Saturday while we were sitting on the stoep wall watching it grow dark, she or I said something that led to something else, which led to a teasing and an exchange of slaps and parries, which led to the rest. Neither of us had really expected it, but afterwards we couldn't understand why it had taken us so long to arrive at that self-evident moment.

She told everybody that she'd taken me because she couldn't find anybody else, and I'd taken her because she couldn't find me anybody else either.

It ended, ultimately, exactly as it had started. Neither of us saw it coming. I just knew one day that that wasn't really what I wanted. It was all just too easy, too comfortable, too simple, too dead ordinary, too self-evident. Unfortunately she did not agree. She wouldn't accept it. And the worst of it was that I couldn't give her a single valid, producible reason.

The rest was rather dismal; days and nights of painful and incoherent conversations full of confused silences and reproaches and tears and words of comfort. Until I knew with absolute finality that the morning train was my only way out, no matter to where.

That was Kristi, whom I'd learnt to love more or less by default. Perhaps I'd known it all along and denied it for selfish reasons. Perhaps I simply outgrew her. Or perhaps Kristi was the chance I let slip through my fingers.

Jenny was something completely different. She was no more than a moment of intoxication. But if she was really no more than that, I wondered over and over from almost the first day, why had she had such a paralysing grip on me almost instantaneously?

She was not particularly pretty. She made a point of dressing like a man and behaving like a man. I had the impression all the time, when I was with her, that she was unaware of me. In spite of the fact that I explained some five times that first day and often again afterwards that my first name was Brand and my surname de la Rey, she persisted in addressing me as Mr Brand.

That morning on the way to Shabeni I had no inkling of what was in store. I was too immersed in my thoughts about the Jock Mills affair. Although it might be possible to make a case that I was already not thinking too clearly by then.

Jenny Grobler evidently didn't know much more about Jock Mills's actions and antics of the previous few days than I. Except that she'd talked to him by telephone and had seen him briefly after that. He and his plane were indeed still in one piece. He was in Manzini where apparently he'd made an emergency landing. They'd refused to let him take off again without radio equipment, and she'd been obliged to borrow money from somebody, buy a radio and go and deliver it to him in Manzini. If the authorities in Swaziland had not in the meantime ruled otherwise, he was on his way back to Shabeni, where it was hoped he would land at eleven o'clock that morning.

His only request was a windsock next to the landing strip so that he could try landing against the wind; for reasons that I could only speculate about, this was apparently of cardinal import.

We were there at half-past ten. Jenny had brought a windsock and the original mast pole was still there – the problem was to climb up the pole and tie the sock up there. A quarter of an hour's thorough search of the base had not produced any ladder other than the two-metre bamboo contrivance with which Mills used to clamber into the Dakota. The pole was at least five metres long and badly rusted, which made the ascent a bit easier. Barefoot, with the sock clenched between my teeth and Jenny as uninvolved spectator, I went up the mast pole.

"You must be careful, Mr Brand, the thing is rocking a lot. I hope it's not rusted through at the bottom."

"Don't hope – look!"

"I'm scared you'll fall on me."

There was a light westerly wind and the piece of cloth flapped all the time between my hands. Perhaps it was the flapping of the sock or the fact that it was approaching downwind, but I saw the plane only when it was six hundred metres from us. There was still no sound. Only the great shiny-grey bird that came floating along, flickering in the heat vibrations. The first audible noise was the high, shrill keening of the propellers, and only then, with the plane scarcely twenty metres above the ground, the droning racket of the engines. I quite forgot to get down off the pole; under the flapping windsock I sat watching Jock Mills bringing his rattling, rickety, lopsided plane down to earth, grudgingly, little by little, almost lovingly and at an angle to the wind.

SEVEN

I

Jock Mills was still in the same khaki pants and shirt in which he'd left three days earlier; the only difference was that his clothes and hands and face were considerably dirtier.

He was visibly tired. I had to help him down the rickety ladder. His beard and hair were grey with dust, as if he'd been travelling on the back of a bakkie on a dirt road. And he smelt powerfully of sweat. And faintly of brandy.

"Good to see you, Jock."

"Good to be back."

"I thought you were going for fifteen minutes."

"I thought you saw my wheel."

"I did."

"On two wheels at a hundred and fifty kilometres an hour an aardvark burrow is a bugger. On one wheel it's more or less…"

Suddenly he saw Jenny and held open his arms. They hugged each other and I could see her tensing up as she said: "Been drinking again, my baby."

"Not to worry."

He was a centimetre shorter than she. And there was a flask of brandy in his back pocket.

"I don't suppose it occurred to you to bring me a hamburger or a pizza?"

Then, for the very first time that morning, Jenny Grobler smiled: "Ag, dammit, how could I forget!"

"Shit, I'm starving."

"Mr Brand probably has something at home."

"De la Rey."

She didn't seem to hear me. She was combing the dust out of Jock's beard and hair with her fingers. "What you need is a proper scrub-down. I did at least bring clean clothing."

There was a kind of comfortable matter-of-factness between the two of them that gave one the impression of an old married couple. I found it profoundly irritating.

The plane's damaged wheel strut had been fixed. "How does she do in the air, Jock?" I was examining the repairs.

"Hundred per cent. OK, make that ninety. A bit of vibration on the wings. But I'll get rid of that. On the way out she was full of hiccups, but much better this morning."

"Hell, you had me worried. I thought you were dead."

"What, you haven't heard anything yet. Wait till I give you the story!"

It was indeed quite a story. On the way back, he gave an account, piecemeal, a bit here and a scrap there, of his travails.

"*You* were worried! You were on the ground, remember. I was two thousand bloody feet in the air!"

When they got into the bakkie, Jock took the flask of brandy from his pocket and took a swig. I saw Jenny reaching for the flask. "Chuck away that stuff, Jock!" But he just slapped her hand away and screwed back the stopper and pushed the flask into his shirt pocket. He was sitting in the middle. Whether this was because he wanted to sit between Jenny and me or she preferred it that way wasn't clear. But along the way, while he was telling his story, he took out the flask every now and again and took another swig. And even for as hard a drinker as Jock, that was rather hard on the stomach. Because as would become evident with time, he hadn't slept for something like three days and in five days had eaten only twice.

The plane would probably have passed its test flight with flying colours, more or less, if it hadn't been for the ant heap that knocked the left wheel just about off its axle. He could just see the damage from the side window, and that radically changed his plan of action on the spot. He would not be able to land at Shabeni again. Even to consider an emergency landing, he'd have to go looking for an airstrip with at least a tarmac surface. And even a tarmac would not spell the end of his problems, because at some stage, two thousand feet above ground, he was prepared for the first time to admit that even had there been two wheels underneath him he'd have been scared to land a brand-new DC-3, never mind a decrepit one full of aches and pains.

There was not enough fuel to shilly-shally or to sit mollycoddling his fears. He'd have to choose straight away: Manzini or Richards Bay or Durban. Durban was too busy for an unscheduled flight without radio contact. Richards Bay would have been an option if only he could remember the day of the week, because over week-ends the place was abuzz with small private craft on pleasure trips. Nelspruit was too far. Maputo was looking for trouble with all its military police and political phobias.

Manzini.

He turned the Dakota north-north-west and noticed that the left aileron was sluggish. The altimeter was acting up and something told him that the right wing was vibrating much more than the left. And he was definitely smelling petrol. He recognized a hamlet underneath him as Big Bend. A few minutes later there was an-other town due west – and that was either Sidvokodvo or he was off course. He scanned the horizon from left to right, from right to left, sedulously looking for beacons, rivers, towns, something that half looked like Manzini.

Manzini was not too long coming. And that was probably just as well, because the petrol smell was now all over the cabin. He spotted the aerodrome straight away. A good long landing strip north-east-south-west and one crossing it north-south. But there was another problem. There was one hell of a lot of traffic. In the three minutes that he circled, no fewer than two planes landed and two took off, and he could see others waiting. He waited for a gap and buzzed the control tower. And made a tight turn and buzzed again. He could see, on the second time round, a small twelve-seater aborting so abruptly that smoke poured from the tarmac. He gave a small Piper a chance to land and buzzed a third time. He could see people crowding around the airport buildings, and a vehicle with flashing emergency lights emerged from a shed and started moving slowly down the north-south strip. After his fifth buzz both strips were clear. The wind was from the west. He approached from the north-east and realized twenty metres from the ground that he was too fast and had to climb again. There were now three emergency vehicles and something that looked like a fire engine. Halfway through another north-east approach, the wind veered south-west and he decreased speed and came in against the wind, trying all the time to land tail end first. But the Dakota didn't want that. She refused to obey instructions. Either she hadn't been built for it or she was too rusty and rickety to do what he asked. There was a moment, suddenly, five metres above the tar – a single flash of absolute clarity – when he realized, as when you see your own hand in front of your face, that this thing that he had to try to control was five times bigger and ten times clumsier than anything he'd ever flown.

It was too late to do anything about this.

He promised himself that he wouldn't shut his eyes. He'd stay in control until something else took over from him. He tried one last time to lift the nose and braked with the right wing to compensate for the absence of a left wheel.

The Dakota struck the tarmac right side first and the next moment the whole world was white with sparks and he was aware of the pain in his neck and arms and there was a hellishly long moment during which it felt as if he was splitting Manzini aerodrome in two.

Then there was silence. And smoke. And something that almost seemed on the point of sounding like the first octave of something or other by Mozart that he couldn't quite place immediately.

And then the sirens.

They arrested him on the spot.

Under normal circumstances Jock hardly ever swore. But even a beer or two had the capacity to expand his vocabulary remarkably. And because he was firmly of the opinion that one could swear more effectively in Afrikaans than in English, he seldom spoke English when he'd downed a few.

While he was recounting his story, and in spite of Jenny's muttered remonstrations, he was laying into his brandy with some gusto. And the consequences started manifesting themselves unmistakably in a remarkable array of strong verbs and adverbs.

He was locked into a little room in the airport building with a whole sheaf of forms to fill in. Through a small barred window he could see them towing away the Dakota by tractor around the building to Heaven knew where. After half an hour somebody came to collect the forms. "So this guy comes in after a while; he looks like a KGB agent – blasted big moustache and sunglasses. He asks for my passport. I don't have a passport. Whose aircraft is it? I say it belongs to the South African army. Aha, so I'm spying. I say has he ever tried spying with a DC-3? He asks what am I doing in Swaziland. I say he should read the blasted forms where I've set out everything neatly and clearly. This guy is still giving me a hard time – when here come the cops. Two fat constables and a sergeant or a brigadier or something with stripes. Dos Santos or somebody. What the hell a Dos Santos is doing in Swaziland he alone knows. But he reckons I've contravened this paragraph number so-and-so of the Law on Civil Aviation. I say, whoa now, just a minute, I'd like to see *you* sitting all law-abidingly waiting for your plane's fuel to run out just because it's against this or that law to land without permission!

"He says they're going to lock me up until they're sure my story about the airlift to Durban is true. Who must they phone? I say I don't know. I say it's a temporary tent settlement somewhere south of Durban. I say I think it's the Red Cross.

"Six o'clock that evening they report back that the Red Cross has never heard of me. They take me down to the cells and give me a plate of cold rice and a blanket and they switch off the light in the passage outside."

The next morning after a long wrangle he got permission to phone Jenny Grobler. She had to find out for him whom the police had to talk to to confirm his story, and she had to bring him radio equipment.

"I'm still talking to her, when here they are again and they take me back to the cells. I think they wanted to eavesdrop while I was talking on the phone, and then they didn't understand Afrikaans. I sweet-talk them and I plead, and I say – because by this time it was a little white woman sergeant, a little fatty with a beard, but she reports that somebody... somebody reports..."

Later Jenny was firmly convinced that he'd fainted, but it's more likely that he'd simply been overtaken by sleep. One moment he was still telling his story, a bit incoherently but still, and the next moment he was fast asleep with his chin on his chest. And not even the bad road and a flat tyre could bring him to consciousness.

Jenny knew the rest of the story first-hand.

She was in Manzini by the next day. With the radio equipment and with the phone numbers of the mission station and the supervisor of the refugee camp in Umbilo. She looked on while the airport police phoned the Umbilo number to corroborate Jock's story. An hour later the man with the KGB moustache came to say that it had been decided not to prosecute Jock and that he could take off on condition that he equipped his plane with a radio.

Who fixed the wheel, and when, and who paid for it, she couldn't say.

Arriving home, I had to carry the sleeping Jock to the bedroom, and Jenny with the best will in the world couldn't wake him to feed him his plate of food.

He slept for the rest of the day.

2

There was quite a bit of work for me to catch up. I got hold of Vukile Khumalo by radio and told him about the Dakota. We would come to inspect the mission station's airstrip the next day and, if it was safe enough by Jock's standards, he'd take the first consignment of people to Durban the following day. I asked myself afterwards why, when Vukile offered to call Julia, I'd been in too much of a hurry to wait for her.

Vusi came to say that there was a kudu bull on the footpath behind the ironstone ridge that was too weak to get up, and that I had to go and shoot. There were others, he said, that wouldn't make the end of the month. He was now finding dead rhebok and bushbuck in the veld every day and three times in a single week he'd had to fetch a carcass in the veld and bury it.

There was activity behind the reed screen of the outside shower next to the house. A spluttering and splashing of water and several other unidentifiable sounds that could suggest blissful indulgence and satisfaction. Jenny's khaki clothes were hanging over the reed enclosure. I was sharpening my skinning knife on the whetstone. The reed enclosure beckoned me enticingly. I knew I shouldn't be doing it, but I walked up to the enclosure until I could see the brown of her body through the reeds. I wanted to get out of there. But I couldn't. I stood looking. I could see her turning round and round under the steaming spray of water. There was a string of big white beads around her waist and either she regularly sunbathed without clothes or she was naturally brown-skinned. Something – a cough, what? – made me realize Vusi was standing five metres behind me, with something that could almost pass for a smile.

"Jenny... Are you... Have you got everything?" That was the best I could do under the circumstances. "Have you got soap?"

"No. Do you?"

The bedroom window was two metres from me. I put my hand through the window and grabbed the soap in the washbasin and held it out to her over the reeds. "Here you are!"

I could see a part of her hip and half of one breast.

She took the cake of soap from me with a wet hand and from the motion of her elbow I could deduce that she was soaping herself.

She did not thank me.

Then I turned round and walked past Vusi. "Come! We've got work to do!"

We went and skinned the kudu without speaking a single word to each other. I loaded the two haunches onto the bakkie and Vusi the head and shoulders. We had to join forces to get the two halves of the ribcage loaded. At home I covered it all with wet sacks.

My shirt was full of blood and my arms smeared with red up to the elbows. I was in a hurry to go and wash myself, but there was no more hot water. It was six o'clock. I went and made a fire under the drum.

Jock Mills was still fast asleep. Somewhere in the house, like a fleeting thought, was the slight redolence of perfume, and a hairbrush on the kitchen table. I opened a bottle of wine, poured myself a glass, and went to sit on the steps of the back stoep. Jenny Grobler was nowhere to be seen.

Strange woman. I couldn't decide how far I should trust my judgement. I was torn between conflicting feelings. Her dark, fixed stare was trying to say something, as was her almost masculine decisiveness, and her vulnerable mouth, her absence and aloofness, her supple walk, her men's clothes and shock of black hair, her almost hostile silences and merry copper bracelets.

Dusk was overtaking the yard, earlier than I'd got used to over that endless summer. I didn't really want to think about it, but it had long since started to seem not just possible but probable that the summer would pass without a single proper shower of rain.

What was Jenny Grobler's case?

I knew I was waiting for something to happen, because my senses told me that something was just waiting for the right moment to happen. I didn't know what. She was restless, and I thought it could be because of Mills, but I wasn't sure.

Malume and his henchmen were in the ficus forest again. They were curious about the strangers on the premises. I think, in fact, it must have been the jingling of Jenny's bracelets that had piqued their interest.

I went to fetch clean clothes and stoked the fire under the drum one last time. The water was hot enough. I was taking off my socks when I saw her standing next to me.

"Are you a bleeder?" she enquired drily.

"Yes."

"What happened?"

"Skinned a kudu."

"I thought you were a wildlife conservationist."

"Something of the kind. But conservation's no use once they've starved to death."

"So some people will be eating biltong again."

"I was hoping we could cut out something that we could cook tonight. But it's only the liver that's still usable."

I was taking off my shirt. That, I thought, would make her clear off. But she didn't. The shirt was heavy with blood; an inexperienced butcher makes more of a mess than a meal. I draped my shirt over the reed enclosure exactly where her shirt had been a while ago. There was a hesitation – then she took a step forward and smelt the shirt. I could see her nostrils flaring for a moment.

"What does it smell like?"

"Blood."

I loosened my belt, my eyes fixed on her. She stood waiting – evidently amused. Then I turned my back on her and stripped off my trousers and walked in behind the screen. "There's cold wine on the back stoep, if you want to drink something in the meantime." I opened the tap wide and walked in under the lukewarm water and waited for it to heat up, watching the dried blood gradually peeling off my arms.

There was a moment, later – it was almost dark – when I suddenly knew that she was standing in the screen opening watching me. And because I didn't know what to do about it, I pretended not to notice.

There was light in the kitchen when I emerged from the shower. The sound of pots and pans meant that Vusi was cooking. The bottle of wine was no longer on the stoep table, but the two glasses were untouched. Jenny Grobler was nowhere to be seen.

I looked out over the yard.

"Are you looking for your wine?" Her voice was somewhere close by.

"Yes." I could now make out her figure, ten metres from me, in a cane chair under the wild olive.

"I put it away."

"Why? Don't you drink wine?"

"Do you want Jock to function tomorrow, or do you want a hungover zombie on your hands?"

"He's sleeping."

"He'll be awake soon."

"Have a glass with me before he wakes up."

"I don't drink."

I went to get the wine out of the fridge, took the two glasses and went to sit with her. "What do you do for a living, Jenny?"

"At the moment nothing to write home about."

"And before that?"

"Whatever came along."

"Like?" I was pouring two glasses. I offered her one. "Like what?" When she neither took the glass nor replied, I looked up.

"I don't drink."

"Sorry. And cheers!"

She crossed her legs a little impatiently and started playing with her bracelets.

"From where do you and Jock Mills know each other?" I asked.

"From the Salvation Army."

"The Salvation Army."

"Yes."

"So you worked for the Salvation Army?"

"No."

"Then what?"

"They looked after me."

She was in no mood to talk.

"Why?"

She sat gazing at her hands for a long time and then looked straight at me. "I had a drinking problem."

"Oh."

Then, perhaps because I didn't continue my interrogation, she smiled and shook her head. "It's no business of mine whether you drink or not. That's your problem. I'm just trying to get Jock not to drink."

"I understand."

"I don't think you do understand. I know all about such things. They picked me up on the beach one New Year's Eve when I didn't even know my own name. So they took me in. I don't think I was older than nineteen."

"And then Jock was there with the same problem?"

"Yes. But by then he was much better. At that point he wasn't drinking at all. He was already playing in their band by then."

"And I suppose he fell head over heels in love with you."

"No, why? We fought like cat and dog. But he was very good to me. He taught me to play the trumpet."

"He can play the trumpet?"

"Trumpet, piano, violin, tuba, the lot. So then I was in the band as well. He always drove the band's minibus. So we travelled up and down from Port Edward all the way to Richards Bay and back and gave beach concerts. And every time that I ran away and took to drinking again, he searched all over the place until he'd found me. Then he helped me get back on my feet all over again. Then as punishment I'd have to help him when the bus broke down. The thing broke down all the time."

"How long did this carry on?"

"Almost three years. Later we'd long given up drinking, then we were still playing in the band. Until he started fixing the Dakota."

"And now he's drinking again."

"Only when things get too much for him. I try to help him. Because if it hadn't been for him, I'd have been a goner long ago."

I drank only one glass of wine and corked the bottle and put it away.

When Jock woke up later that evening he was his old subdued self again. And hungry. Jenny made him wash and put on clean clothes and made me promise not to drink in front of him. We ate on the back stoep, in spite of which Vusi wouldn't sit with us. He claimed he wasn't hungry, but we could all see him smuggling a plate of food into his room.

It was stuffy and except for a few crickets somewhere the night was dead silent. Once I thought I heard the baboons, but I wasn't sure; the rest of the time it was just our own voices and the clinking of cutlery.

"Is there nothing to drink, Brand?" Jock demanded at some point. "Have you run out of brandy?"

"You drank the last bit in the bottle yourself."

"You usually have at least a bit of wine somewhere."

"We've got a long day ahead of us tomorrow."

On the face of it Jock was content. But I could see him peeping at Jenny on the sly and smiling. "What time do we have to get going if we want to be at Mbabala before sunrise?"

"Half-past four."

"Then we start at half-past four. If the landing strip seems OK, I want to go and do a few more things to the plane. Jenny can take me." She shook her head. "I'm leaving tomorrow."

"Where to?"

"Home."

"Please. Help us just for tomorrow. You can leave on Wednesday." It was a trick of hers not to reply, to leave you guessing what she was thinking. She generally avoided your eyes; but when she did look at you, it was straight into your eyes as if she was trying to see all the way into the back of your head. That evening on the back stoep by the dim light of the two lanterns I watched her constantly – her restless hands, her mop of dark hair, her evasive eyes, the narrow wings of her nose that flared abruptly every now and again when somebody said something not to her taste.

In all that evening she only once looked straight at me. We'd finished eating and I was lighting a third lantern. "We'll have to figure out who sleeps where," I said. "There's a couch and one bed and an extra mattress." The dark look she gave me was somewhere between indignation and boredom. I didn't look away. "I think you should take the bed," I said. "Jock and I can sleep in the sitting room."

"As you wish."

Vusi's room was dark already. I went and knocked at his window and spoke to him through the glass. "We have to get up at four o'clock, Vusi."

"Yes."

"I'm sleeping on the floor in the sitting room."

"Yes."

The butcher's knives were still lying outside next to the tap. I rinsed them and slid them in under the eaves of the roof.

It was too dark to be absolutely sure, but judging by his size it must have been Malume. He was sitting in the second fork of the dead bushwillow next to the hot-water drum, five or six metres from me. I took one step nearer to him, and then another, and a third, but he just sat motionlessly watching me. It was only when after a long while I took a fourth step that he slowly lowered himself to the first fork and sauntered off without looking at me.

I slept on the mattress on the floor, Jock on the couch, Jenny on the single bed in my room. Jock slept like a log; I hardly at all. And all night I could hear her tossing and turning. I heard her drink water in the kitchen. I heard her go out by the back door, heard her returning and lying down and getting up again, rooting in the pantry. Once she came to kneel by Jock's bed. She tried to wake him, but he wouldn't respond. The moon was bright outside and in the block of light streaming in through the window, I could see her body crouched darkly in the unnatural light. I turned on my back and watched her.

"Jenny?" She either didn't hear me or ignored me – and yet, eventually, came to crouch by me too. I could see her brown kneecaps and the dark shadow disappearing between her legs. She put her hand on my chest and slid it down to my stomach. And got to her feet and disappeared into the room next door. But when I followed her, against my better judgement, short of breath, a lamb to the slaughter, and sat down on the bed next to her, she turned away and lay stiff-backed waiting for me to clear off.

That must have been long after midnight. The black-backed jackal called again once far away in the hills. A hopeless, godforsaken sound.

The following day, Wednesday, I suspected, would bring clarity on many a matter.

3

Gwaja's airstrip, as it was straight away dubbed, was a remarkable piece of work. It was now sixty paces wide and easily a thousand of Gwaja's paces long.

Because the surroundings were flat, it had been necessary only to dig up shrubs, cut the grass and remove ant heaps. But with the labour at his disposal, it was astonishing what he'd achieved within a single week.

There was even a windsock: the tattered remains of the hospital's ironing sheet knotted to a long stick tied high up in the top of a fever tree.

"What do you think, Jock?" an out-of-breath Vukile demanded, exhausted from the rapid pace at which Jock was measuring out the airstrip.

"Excellent." He stopped. "Absolutely. Couldn't ask for anything better than this."

"What a relief! Hell, boy, wonderful. We really need to get rid of these people now. Really."

Jock started pacing off the strip again, but Vukile was unaware of this. He just carried on talking. And all that Jock could do was to leave him behind. This was not difficult, because although Vukile was considerably thinner than normal, he was not fit in any case and he was prone to a tightness of the chest – and that morning, for the first time since I'd known him, his breath smelt of brandy.

Julia was still asleep that morning when we arrived, because she'd been on duty till midnight. On our return from inspection there was still no sign of her. Nor of Jenny, who on our arrival had immediately taken off on her own.

We were on the large screened-in front stoep of the hospital – Jock, Vukile and I, each with a large glass of water. It was seven o'clock and already so hot that one laboured to breathe. Everybody held a hand over his glass of water, because the stoep was full of cheeky flies constantly walking all over everybody's faces and crawling into one's ears and shirtsleeves.

They agreed that Vukile would arrange with the camp in Umbilo for them to offload the first consignment of forty people at Durban airport before eight the next morning. The earlier, the less turbulence there would be. If everything went smoothly, they'd consider a second flight, and perhaps more passengers, depending on how the Dakota handled its first shipment of forty.

According to Vukile there had been, at last count, the previous afternoon, just over three hundred and fifty people on the premises, of whom something like eight would probably not survive the day. But for every death there were on average three new arrivals per day. Two flights a day would mean that by Sunday all the refugees would be in Durban. So, from next week, depending on the rate of new arrivals, one or two flights a week should be enough.

Jenny came in from outside. She was visibly upset. "Hell, Jock," she said, and sat down on the nearest chair. "You didn't tell me it was this bad."

"Why do you think we're trying to get them to the Red Cross?"

"Yes, but there are dead people lying around here! They just leave them like that!" She had that strange fixed glint in her eye again.

"There's only one old nun who—"

"What is she talking about?" Vukile couldn't understand her Afrikaans, but he could see she was distressed.

"Some of them seem to have been dead for days."

"The people aren't keeping up," I tried to explain, though I suspected she was exaggerating.

Vukile's puzzled eyes were darting from Jenny to Jock to me.

"What's the problem?"

"Are you asking me?" She was on her feet suddenly. "What the… How do you think you… Are you a doctor?"

"Yes."

"Shit!"

"What is she talking about?"

"If you can't save their lives, for God's sake, then at least bury them!"

"You want to help us?" A strangled sound escaped Vukile's throat, half hysterical laughter and half crying, his eyes screwed up as if he was staring straight into the sun. "You want a shovel? You want to start digging? I'll give you a shovel!"

She was on her way out, with Vukile in pursuit.

"I'll give you a fucking shovel! I'll give you two shovels; you can dig two graves at a fucking time!"

I stopped him at the door and gripped his wrist. "Wait, Vukile. Just wait a minute, please."

"Who the hell does she think she is?" He abruptly yanked his wrist from my grip. "Who is she anyway?" He was clearly not really interested in knowing, because he was already on his way back into the building. I tried to follow him, but he slammed the door to the ward behind him.

I went outside. I realized all of a sudden that I hadn't seen any of the staff other than Vukile.

Jock Mills was trying to calm Jenny down on the other side of the bakkie. Gwaja was nowhere to be seen. The kitchen was empty. Both coal stoves were cold. Sister Roma appeared in the back door for a moment and then vanished again like a phantom.

There was smoke in the cooking shelter and I could smell burnt mealie porridge.

I went to Julia's place. She was lying asleep in a dirty uniform. Her face was much leaner than normal, she was as pale as wax and her hair was tangled as if she'd not washed it for a long time. I picked up the pillow from the floor and tried to tidy her sheets, but they were hanging halfway to the floor.

Something was wrong.

I went to sit next to her hoping that she would wake up. She did not.

I sat gazing at her face. I couldn't hear her breathing. But her lower lip was trembling slightly.

There was a sound at the back door. From where I was sitting on the bed, I could see Vukile coming in. But gingerly. As if he wasn't sure that he belonged there. He advanced to a step beyond the bedroom door and stopped there.

"Brother." He wasn't addressing me or asking a question; he simply wanted to announce his presence.

"How long has she been sleeping?"

"Since yesterday."

"What time yesterday?"

"Morning."

"What's wrong with her?"

"She's tired."

"Where is Gwaja? Where is Sister Erdmann? Why is Sister Roma acting so strangely?"

"They are tired."

"And you?"

Vukile had probably not expected the question. He was caught somewhat unawares. He sat down on his haunches. And suddenly started crying. But it wasn't just crying. He was a man of over forty with a history of his own. An unknown history of which only he knew the totality. It was perhaps years of suppressed emotions, the sobs of many years that in one sudden rush sought to break through his clenched lips. He had tried hard, with bitter courage, to keep everything trapped within himself, but now he suddenly could no longer. It was possibly the first time in many years that someone had for a fraction of a second shown the slightest interest in how *he* was. He had not expected it. The spit and mucus exploded from his mouth and nose in a single blast of air, and I had to watch him sitting on his haunches in the doorway and crying like a little boy.

"What is wrong, Vukile?"

He battled to regain control over himself. "What is wrong?" The harder he tried, the less self-control there was. "You ask me what's wrong?"

"I know what's wrong. But it's not your fault. You've been trying your best. I know. It's not fair, Vukile, I know."

"I sedated her. All of them. I've been sedating them since Sunday. I was trying to save them. Please, for God's sake, brother – those who are dying, let them die. I want to save the rest of us."

"*Ja.* I know. I understand."

"I'm not a very good doctor. Whoa, it's time you knew that. But I… Yeah, I can fight disease. I can handle it. But I can't handle people dying of hunger. I can't handle God."

I hunkered down in front of Vukile and placed my hand on his shoulder. "By next Sunday all of them will be gone. I promise you. We'll take them away."

It was as if Vukile did not hear me. His head was in another place.

"I can't handle God. What happened to God? Where the fuck did the rain go, brother? What happened to the rain?"

I went to tell Jock that I wasn't prepared to leave Julia like that. I wanted to be there when she woke up. Jenny should take him to Shabeni in my bakkie. I'd be waiting for him next morning on Gwaja's landing strip.

I sat by Julia all the time to make sure that Vukile did not inject her again. She woke up now and again, but dropped off again immediately. Once she asked for water. Her trembling lips bothered me and I went to look for Vukile. He wasn't in the hospital. There was nobody in the hospital. Sister Roma was cooking soup in the reed shelter. She was more stooped and smaller and blacker than I remembered her.

"*Yebo, mama. Kunjani?*"

"*Sikhona, mnumzane.* It is well." It was the first time she'd ever addressed me as *mnumzane*.

"Are you holding out, *mama*?"

"The Lord keeps me upright."

"Where are all the others?"

"They're resting a bit. They need it."

"Do you know where Vukile is?"

"I think you must go and look in his house. He is not well."

Vukile's front door was open. The little sitting room was woefully untidy. The bathroom tap was leaking and the toilet was flowing non-stop. His bedroom door was closed. I knocked, but there was no reply. I opened the door gently and saw Vukile lying on the bed. There was a syringe and a glass with brandy on the cabinet next to the bed. It didn't look as if he was going to wake up any time soon.

Outside things were remarkably quiet for so many people. Everybody sat in the meagre shade of trees and branch shelters gazing in front of them, quiet and resigned, as if accepting that they'd been overtaken by fate. They no longer as in the beginning looked up into my eyes as if I were a messiah.

On my way back to Julia's *kaya* I saw Gwaja and somebody else hobbling along with a body on a litter. The person had been dead for a long time. He was lying on his back with his arms and legs bent upwards as if he'd been turned to stone while trying to stop something running past him.

For the rest of the morning I helped Sister Roma with the cooking and in the afternoon helped dig graves.

Julia slept all day.

At sundown I went and washed and I latched the back door and fell asleep on a few cushions in front of Julia's bed.

And while I slept, I knew all the time that the next day, Thursday, would be D-Day.

EIGHT

I

According to Mills it was more or less twenty minutes' flight from Shabeni to Mbabala. The arrangement was that Jock would take off at daybreak; he could then reach the mission station by six at the latest. But at six there was still no sign of him. By seven the day was like an oven already; the horizon all round shimmered like a lake. By nine the light was quaking white as if the earth were glowing with heat. The kind of turbulence that went with such heat might have given Jock second thoughts. At eleven a wind started blowing from somewhere as if straight from hell; a gusty wind that churned tumbleweeds and dust funnels into the air until the sun was no more than a hazy glow somewhere above the storm.

The two nuns went to assemble the people outside and brought them into the hospital, into the church and the little packing shed and the stockrooms that used to be the school. Gwaja and I helped to carry those who could no longer walk.

The wind subsided slightly a few times and then started up again from another direction. Every time with renewed fury.

We looked on with growing concern as one little branch shelter after the other was picked apart; as scraps of cloth and cowhide and ragged blanket detached themselves from the structures and took off over the roofs. The cooking screen slowly but surely gave way, toppling and eventually collapsing against the kitchen wall. A while later Gwaja's ironing sheet was yanked from the fever tree and disappeared over the church roof, with its black scorch patches and all. From one of the bare branches that used to be the papaya forest in front of Julia's bedroom window, something was fluttering that looked like Sister Erdmann's bib.

It goes without saying that there was no sign of Jock Mills and his Dakota.

Jenny Grobler was to have driven my bakkie to Mbabala as soon as Jock was airborne. That she hadn't arrived yet could mean either that he had never taken off, or that the route was blocked somewhere by a fallen tree. This also meant that I was stranded. That is, if you were to discount Vukile's 1962 Cortina – which would be prudent, because Vukile had given up trying to keep it going two years previously.

The good news was that both Julia and Vukile were more or less back on their feet again. Julia pale and shaky and still slightly discombobulated, and Vukile down at the mouth and constantly looking the other way as if somebody had caught him red-handed. He went to stand on the hospital stoep looking at the wind savaging the trees and hurling loads of dry leaves and dead beetles and millipede husks against the gauze screen.

It was difficult to move about in the over-full rooms. Wherever you ended up in there, you had to stay put, waiting for the storm to subside. Vukile and I were close together. Julia and the nuns were nowhere to be seen, but Gwaja, who was still pottering about outside, came to signal through the screen that they were in the kitchen. He passed by the stoep every now and again, bearing into the wind or tottering downwind with a spade or a three-legged pot or a bucket that he'd gone to salvage somewhere.

After a while I shuffled cautiously down the passage, went out by a side door and ran around to the kitchen to go and look for Julia. It was more difficult than I'd anticipated; it was as if the wind was trying to blow my legs from under me – I had to remain close to the building all the time, close to the walls, trying to stay out of the way of the fiercest gusts.

From outside I could see Julia standing by a window, her forehead pressed to the pane, gazing out as if not really seeing anything, not even me – until I was right in front of her.

She went to open the screen door for me and we stood in the doorway watching the dust and dislodged clumps of grass and leaves being driven up against the church roof.

"I think I should sit down," she said after a while. "My stomach is feeling queasy."

"I'll take you home."

"Please."

We tried to run, but the wind was blowing too hard. There was too much sand and dust in the air to see just where we were going, but we could hear the kitchen's screen door and a window slamming in the wind all the time. The cloth from the kitchen table had been blown into the sitting room and everywhere in the house glasses and vases and glass picture frames were lying smashed on the floor.

We cleared up without talking much. It was as if the wind constantly claimed our undivided attention. Whoever was talking, the other was listening with only half an ear – there was the perpetual din of branches breaking and falling on roofs, trees being uprooted and flattening smaller trees, roof timbers groaning, windows shattering somewhere.

"It's not just the humans who are messing with the earth," Julia said when after a while we went to stand at the kitchen window watching the trees bent double.

"I suppose not."

There was something overwhelming, something totally terrifying in this unusual demonstration of elemental whimsy. I moved from window to window gaping at the violence. I knew the wind was blowing away months of my work. But the gale was as valid a phenomenon as all the others that I'd been documenting for so long. Just as valid, just as inexplicable and apparently just as essential a part of what I'd represented to myself as the Great Process.

That deep concealed place to which everything is connected and where everything interlocks and from which everything radiates in invisible trajectories may be unreachably far. My purpose had always been gradually to learn to understand more of the cohesion of all the disparate elements of nature. Somewhere, someday, research would bring us to the symbiosis that contains all things. The drought was destroying the little that conservation had achieved in fifty years in the region. Was there a reason for this or was it just happening because it was happening? The little that I knew had time after time confirmed that nature had no use for chance. Theologians would talk of a Divine Plan – but that was not what I meant by my Great Process, even though I did spell it with capital letters, and even though it could be one and the same thing. But too many people tend to place the so-called Divine Plan stamp on everything they don't understand and then regard it as settled. Every flood, every epidemic and drought and earthquake is part of the Process and as such it is research material. The dust storm was also a part of it. I tried to look at the storm as if through the lens of a microscope or a camera, but I didn't succeed.

At three o'clock that afternoon, when the wind died down at last, it was in the blink of an eye, as if a door had been slammed in the face of some low-pressure system.

The afternoon was suddenly dead quiet. When I went outside, the yard was bare and red and lifeless under my feet. No sign of life remained in the bush surrounding the hospital. Those trees that were left standing had been stripped of their leaves. The sky was a red dome of dust suffocating all beneath it, red-brown and dark in the east and gradually lightening to orange towards the sunset side. At more or less four o'clock one could make out the glow in the west where the sun was supposed to be. There was no sign of a bird or an insect or even an ant. On the airstrip the remaining grass balanced dead still on wind-stripped roots as if trying to stand on stilts. Gwaja was dragging severed branches and toppled trees off the runway and I helped him.

We were still doing that when I saw my bakkie approaching through the trees from the hospital. It was Jenny – grey with dust and covered in oil stains.

"How do you manage to drive a bakkie like that?" were her first words.

"Why?"

"The thing's falling to pieces."

"Funny. It's got two hundred thousand on the clock and it's never broken down."

"It won't break down. It will simply subside into a puddle of oil. On my way here I had to set the points and the carburettor and clean the spark plugs and tighten the fan belt."

"Thank you." I could hear the engine was idling a bit more smoothly.

"What's happened to Jock?"

"He and Vusi are coming."

"He and *Vusi*?"

"They were supposed to take off at five."

"He and Vusi?"

But there was no time for her to explain. From out of the dusky bank of dust the sound suddenly broke through like thunder. We looked up and saw something like lightning. But it was not lightning. It was a tiny bit of sunshine flashing off the Dakota's front window. The plane was approaching from the south-east, very slowly, like a great ship being brought to land on a tranquil sea through the last swells.

Gwaja was in the middle of the runway gesticulating and shouting commands: "*Nkosiyame! Nkosiyame!* Wait, we're not ready for you! Stop, *mnumzane! Stop!*"

There were still branches and other detritus on the landing strip. Not a lot, but enough to be dangerous. And Jock must have seen it, because he lifted the nose of the Dakota and started climbing again and went to circle at a distance while Gwaja and Jenny and I ran around frantically dragging off branches. In a second and a third low fly-by Jock came to check on our progress. The Dakota's engines were sounding good, the wheels were in place, the wings were level, even the wing and tail lights were pulsing. Then at last, very softly and cautiously, as one does with a shy young woman, he came in through the bare trees almost apologetically and hardly raised a puff of dust when his wheels touched ground.

2

Not that there was much to eat, but of the little that there was, the few of us tried to make a banquet that evening. Sister Roma baked a bread and opened a few tins of peas and baked beans and conjured up from somewhere canned peaches and dried guava. Vukile's contribution was a bottle of red wine that apparently had been left over from Christmas. Gwaja set the long table in the kitchen as they'd always done formerly, and everyone took a seat. Everyone except Vusi. He was lying, as sick as a dog, in Gwaja's room, recovering from his maiden flight.

Vukile was pouring everybody a thimbleful of wine.

"OK, Jock, so tomorrow is the day!"

"Tomorrow sunrise."

"Can we drink on that?"

"Sure as hell."

Jenny was trying to signal to Jock don't, please don't.

"What?"

She just shook her head.

"Why not?"

I could see her nostrils suddenly dilating.

"You must be joking! One glass of wine! You trust me or not?" Then Vukile lifted his glass. "To Operation Mbabala, ladies and gentlemen."

Julia was holding out her glass to Jock so they could clink. "To Jock Mills!"

"And his DC-3."

Jenny didn't drink her wine and took part in the conversation only when one of the nuns addressed her.

The next day's programme was thrashed out in detail over the meal. The plane's fuel tanks were more or less full. That was enough for two flights. They would try to start loading the passengers an hour before sunrise. It was literally a matter of loading, since most of the passengers were too weak to mount the home-made roof ladder on their own; they'd have to be carried up and loaded one by one. Jock decided to limit the first consignment to forty-five. They'd have to try to take off as soon as possible after first light. After that Vusi and I would fetch a bakkie-load of fuel from Shabeni.

"Who's going to be flight assistant?" I asked. "I take it Vusi is disqualified."

"Not to worry." Jock's hand was on Jenny's shoulder. "We have an experienced one on call."

"What?" Jenny was talking to Sister Erdmann, but she heard at once what Jock was saying. "Definitely not me."

"You promised!"

"No! I said I would help only for today. Do you remember? I wanted to leave yesterday already, Jock. I think you are chancing your arm."

Jock's smile was a secret between him and me. "Leave it to me," was more or less what I could read from the movements of his lips.

Julia and Jenny never spoke to each other all evening. It was noticeable, earlier when they'd sat down at the table, that Jenny first checked where Julia was sitting before finding a seat at the opposite end of the table. They sat taking turns to inspect each other, and then more or less simultaneously decided to ignore each other.

"Great pilots always go to bed early," Jock said at one stage and got up. "Where am I sleeping?"

There was a quick exchange of glances between Sister Roma and Julia and Vukile before Julia decided to take the initiative. "Jock, you and Jenny can sleep in my place."

"Where do you sleep?" I demanded.

"I'm working night shift. We'll devise something for you. Perhaps in Vukile's office. Is that OK with you, Vukile?"

"Whatever." He wasn't sure exactly what Julia had said, but in principle he was in accord.

Suddenly Jenny was standing in front of me. "If you don't mind, I think I'd rather sleep in your bakkie."

"Jenny, come off it!" That was Jock.

I took my key from my pocket and handed it to her. "If you have the time, you can fit new rings."

She went out without saying goodnight to anybody.

Julia went to fetch me an old, lumpy coir mattress from somewhere and suggested that I should bed down behind Vukile's desk. Blankets weren't necessary because the night was stuffy, but I wished I could filch a sheet somewhere – the mattress was centuries old and dusty, which was bad enough, but on top of that it smelt of a few decades' worth of pain and death sweat.

Julia was going to bring tea after her rounds, but I fell asleep and woke up again only after midnight. There was a lit lantern and a cup of cold tea next to my head, and a fierce argument somewhere outside. I got up and went out onto the stoep to hear better, and after a while recognized Jock's voice, and later Jenny's. There was a light in Julia's sitting room. On my way there I could make out Julia's silhouette in the hospital's side door.

"What's going on there?"

"I don't know. She charged off in your bakkie a while ago, but sounds as if she's back."

As I got closer I could hear that Jock had been drinking. Or perhaps, like me, he was still half asleep.

Jock was sitting in his underpants on Julia's bed and Jenny was standing at the foot. "So what the hell were you doing there this time of night? I thought great pilots went to bed early."

"You don't understand a thing, man. You always just see the arse end of everything."

"Yes, of you too!"

I wanted to clear my throat to attract attention, but Jock saw me at once. "Hey, Brand, come and talk to this woman. I'm trying to get a good night's sleep, but she keeps on pestering me."

Jenny's nostrils flared for a moment. "Ag, fuck you, man!" Then she swung around to me. "There you are, Mr Brand, he's yours. A drunken pilot for Operation Mbabala!"

The next moment she was out by the door.

"Have you been drinking, Jock?"

"Yip."

"Why?"

"Worry."

"Ah, bullshit."

"I knew she wouldn't understand. But I thought you would."

There was half a bottle of whatever next to his bed. It smelt like rum.

"Tell me, I'm listening."

"I didn't want to drink. I wanted to come to bed. As God is my witness. When I got to the plane, the thing was packed with fucking people."

"What kind of people?"

"Barutsis. Thingamabobs. Watusis. Masai. What do you call that lot? They got in by themselves. They're fucking sitting and waiting for the sun to fucking rise! They can hardly walk – they've never fucking flown – but they climb the ladder and sit and wait for tomorrow!"

"Are you joking, Jock, or what?"

"Go and have a look."

"So what were you doing there? If you really wanted to go to bed?"

"I wanted to go to bed."

"In the plane?"

"That's where I've been sleeping for the last two years when I'm not at home." He stretched out his hand determinedly to the bottle, reconsidered and dropped it again. "If you want me to fly tomorrow, you must leave me in peace so I can sleep!" He was irritated all of a sudden. In a hopeless situation like his, he probably realized, attack was better than defence.

"You still haven't told me why you started drinking."

"What the hell does it matter? I had a drink. What's so damned terrible about that? I got the fright of my fucking life, if you really must know. When I got there and switched on the torch all I could see were eyes staring at me. Saying help us – take us

153

away! So I took a nightcap. Now everybody's shitting themselves about it."

"Half a bottle of rum is not a nightcap, Jock."

Jock Mills lost his temper one last time. He probably decided that it was time to go on the offensive. He got to his feet, stood bolt upright for a moment as if to make absolutely sure that he could keep his balance, and then toppled forward like a pole.

I didn't help him up. I took the bottle of rum, blew out the candle, and shut the bedroom door behind me.

There was no sign of Jenny anywhere. Julia had also vanished into thin air. It was something after one. I took Vukile's torch and walked towards the airstrip. There were some thirty, forty people sitting under the plane on the bare ground blinking like birds woken up from sleep.

"What are you doing here?" I demanded. Nobody answered. "Is there somebody here who understands Zulu?"

"I understand a bit," somebody replied.

"Why are you all sitting here?"

"We're waiting for the machine to fly."

"You're going to be waiting for a long time. He's only flying tomorrow."

"We will wait."

"Are there people up there?" I pointed at the plane.

"There are."

The rickety wooden ladder with which Gwaja normally cleaned the gutters and windows had been erected next to the fuselage, and the door was open. I mounted the ladder and shone the torch into the cabin. Jock had not lied or exaggerated. There was a whole crowd of people in the plane, twice as many as a DC-3 could carry. They sat on each other's laps, sat in the aisle, in the cockpit, in the open baggage hold at the back – a bank of black skulls staring at the light motionlessly as if the torch hypnotized them.

It was stuffy in that place. All the faces were shiny with sweat. I felt I couldn't breathe. The little air that was there was heavy with the odour of decomposition. It looked as if not one of them would ever stir again – even the teeming flies did not make them bat an eye. They sat gazing in front of them like stuffed owls.

Julia and Vukile and I had speculated more than once whether we'd ever get the people to fly. We had devised plans to persuade them even to get close to the plane, never mind get into it. That was all of a sudden not a problem any more. The problem was how to get half of them out of the plane.

Back in Vukile's office, with the lamp blown out, I tried to forget the staring faces and the flies. But I could not. The dark was too dark to my liking and the sour mattress and dusty floor were too close to my face. I groped around in the dark for the bottle of rum and in the process knocked over the cup of cold tea. I found the bottle and unscrewed the cap and smelt at it and took a swig. A large swig. And then another.

D-Day, I decided, would unfortunately have to be postponed by a day.

3

Julia later maintained that they'd wanted to give me an opportunity to sleep a bit longer, but I was sure that in the confusion they'd forgotten about me. When I woke up at six o'clock, the hospital was almost entirely deserted – only a few patients who were too weak to move had remained behind. Everybody was on the airstrip. And Jock was warming up the Dakota's engines.

Vukile was up in the doorway struggling to help somebody down to the ladder. When I gesticulated at him in an attempt to find out what was happening, his only reaction was to make big eyes at me.

Julia was at the lower end of the ladder. "Morning. I thought I'd let you sleep for a while."

"Julia, that man can't fly."

"He says he can."

"The hell with what he says."

"Then stop him if you can. I tried. Vukile also thinks he can."

It sounded as if Vukile and Jock were arguing, but the engines made too much of a racket to make out what it was about.

"What are they squabbling about?"

"There are still ten people who must get off – they're too scared to get off while the propellers are turning, and Jock doesn't want to cut the engines; he says he's late as it is."

"Where is Jenny?"

"I thought she was sleeping with you."

"With me? Are you mad?"

I tried to help the man down the ladder, but he dug in his heels and it ended in a tussle to get him to the ground. Gwaja was forcing somebody else down. She was protesting vehemently and a few times it was touch and go or both she and Gwaja would have tumbled to the ground. It was only when Gwaja pushed her into my arms so that I could get her down that I saw it was the woman with the red beads. She recognized me too. "Please!" she kept wailing. "Please, God, please! Please!" I wished I could exchange her for somebody else, but I was obliged to drag her to the ground, because behind her there were another two or three on their way down.

There were fewer people in the passenger cabin than the previous night, but still hopelessly too many to take off with. Jock was in the cockpit pushing and pulling and adjusting and turning his dozens of knobs and switches.

"Jock, talk to me."

"Talk. I can hear you."

"I want your attention, Jock."

"I'm busy, for Chrissake, can't you see?"

"You can't fly."

For a moment he dropped everything he was doing and looked up at me. "Why not?" Despite the dark fume of sweating bodies the rum breath hit me in the face like a can of worms.

"You drank too much last night. You can't take this crowd of people—"

"I want another ten passengers off. You have five minutes to do it. Where's Jenny?"

"She's vanished."

"Somebody must come along to help with the passengers. Five minutes and I close that door. I'm taking off at a quarter past and that's absolutely and definitely final!"

Julia and Vukile had now also joined us.

"I'll go along," Julia said.

"No."

"Then who?"

"I'm afraid I am needed at the hospital."

This was not the first time that Vukile Khumalo had joined an Afrikaans conversation as if he'd followed every word.

"No, Vukile." Julia was shaking her head vehemently. "You can't go. I'll go."

That was when I knew that I had no choice. I would have to go. The details escaped me completely later on. If I were to tell, step by step, what happened and how in those next few hours, I'd have to tell a different story with every repetition. Because for a start my head didn't go along, it was left behind on the ground. All that accompanied me was a heart beating panic-stricken somewhere in my throat.

The bumping, vibrating, careening Dakota was halfway down the runway when I was still trying to get the door to shut. The bolt refused to stay in place. It slipped out again and again. I heard Jock shouting to get the passengers away from him, and when I looked round, there were three, four, five of them on their knees on either side of Jock trying to see out of the front window. A few passengers were jostling each other in the aisle, because some wanted to crawl under the seats and others wanted to look out and a few dazed souls wanted to get off the plane. There was a moment when I imagined that the plane was airborne, but the next moment the branches of a young sweet-thorn disintegrated as the wing struck it. The plane veered left and aimed diagonally across the strip with one wheel in the air and the other on the ground, and then there was a growth of guarrie bushes being split asunder and then blue sky to the right and the tops of thorn trees to the left below us. Most of the time Jock wasn't looking where he was flying, he was pushing and pulling at his controls and the plane was either responding to it or trying in spite of it to do precisely what it wanted to. The moment that is most vivid in my memory is me lying on my back with someone at an angle over me, right behind Jock's chair, trying to get to my feet and trying at the same time to thread my belt out of my pants, because the outside door's bolt was on the point of sliding open and I couldn't think of anything other than my belt to secure it.

I had déjà vu about the whole situation. I'd been here before. It had all happened before. It was a nightmare I'd been dreaming since before my birth, exactly as it was taking place now. I knew it all. I just didn't know the ending. There'd never been an ending before.

All the time I recalled how Julia had tried to stop me. Up to the moment I closed the door, she'd maintained that she wanted to go along. She felt it to be part of her duty; it was her job; it was the responsibility of the mission hospital to get the people to Durban. Not mine. I was an outsider. But that was too easy an argument. If it had been valid, Vukile should have gone along. He was the doctor. He'd been trained to deal with such crises. He was after all the responsible functionary. But Vukile and Gwaja and Sister Roma had their hands full keeping the spectators at a distance. Julia only started climbing down the ladder when Jock threatened to take off from under her ladder. "We're late, Julia. We have to take off," he said again and again.

"Get off now, we're late!"

"Late for what?"

"The hotter it gets, the more bumpy the ride!"

"Then we're both going along."

"No. We've already got too many people on board, dammit!"

She was going to say something more, but Jock started pushing up the revs. The engines whined so loudly that one couldn't hear what she was saying any more. She climbed down and removed the ladder herself, but I could see she was still protesting. The plane started moving even before I could slide shut the door.

Jock was talking by radio. I couldn't hear what the other party was saying, but whatever it was, it managed to work Jock up even more.

We were flying much too low for my comfort, and it sounded as if that was exactly what Jock and the control tower were arguing about.

"I can't get any higher, I told you that, for fuck's sake," he was shouting at one stage. "Because of the overload, because of... I dunno, because..."

There had been at least one passenger on each seat before we took off, some sitting on each other's laps, a few on the floor. But we were scarcely in the air before all of them were lying in a heap, scrabbling about in the back of the plane. I tried to get them back into their seats by ones and twos, but it wasn't easy; it cost me at least twenty minutes of hard work to get them more or less settled. I tried to count them, but it was difficult, because the plane dropped a few metres every so often or swerved sideways so that everybody staggered all over the place.

We were flying over a grey landscape all the time, the greyness interrupted only now and again by the dry bed of a river or a thin white line of road or little circles of houses and cattle enclosures. Here and there a shining corrugated-iron roof reflected the light, and once a little cluster of roofs with trees and streets.

I was watching the propellers, and Jock, and the wings in particular. The even drone of the engine was reassuring, and even Jock's constant fiddling with the bunch of controls in front of him was in order. But the wings bothered me. It seemed to me as if they were buckling all the time. It was as if they collapsed upwards and then regained their shape and then collapsed again.

There was a town somewhere that looked like Babanango.

The rest consisted of blocks of dead loam soil that must have been farmland previously and banks of dust and empty corrugated-iron dams. The south was evidently in much worse shape than our remote corner in the north.

I crawled on all fours to Jock and asked him where we were.

"Dunno! But don't worry." I could not figure out what that was supposed to mean.

"Everything OK with you, Jock?"

"Why?"

"Just asking."

"Oil pressure."

"What about the oil pressure?"

His only response was a vague hand gesture which was probably meant to indicate so-so.

By this stage most of the passengers were airsick. Those who could find an open spot stood convulsing on all fours on the floor, but all that they could produce were long strings of slime. Some of the others sat clinging to each other or tried to gag their mouths with their hands. The bravest few just sat dead still and ashen, staring straight ahead of them.

I recognized Greytown. I could feel that the plane was not trying to climb any more; the high whining of the engines changed to a restful murmur. But I could see that Jock was worried. His eyes were nailed to the control panel.

"Is everything in order, Jock?"

"Sort of."

"The engines sound OK. Or not?" He didn't reply.

"What's the oil pressure doing now?"

"That's what I'm trying to find out."

By and by the sea appeared to the left on the horizon. The Durban beachfront was something unreal on an unknown planet – bathers in the breakers, blue umbrellas, the shiny roofs of cars. We swerved inland and curved back to the airport and circled twice, Jock ranting all the time on his radio, vehemently protesting, ever more irritably searching for the right Afrikaans swear words. We circled for a third and fourth time over the hills and suddenly started unmistakably descending over the bushes and shiny roofs and smoking chimneys. I couldn't make out a single word of what the scratchy radio voice was saying. But from the short staccato sentences and the high pitch of the voice and the increasing number of words per minute I could deduce that the control tower was not exactly planning a welcoming party for us. The reason was obvious. There was heavy traffic on all the runways and certainly no space for us to land. I grabbed hold of Jock's backrest and tried to keep my eyes shut, but I couldn't. I had to see. I wanted to witness the end of the nightmare. The Dakota was descending crookedly and shakily over a tarmac full of passenger buses and tractors and scurrying people in yellow overalls. The voice from the control tower was still barking hysterically at one moment and then went silent just as the DC-3 hit the tarmac and bounced once like a very old tennis ball and covered the rest of the distance in little half-hearted hops to come to a standstill fifty metres beyond the tarmac.

Jock turned the plane round and started taxiing back to the terminal building. There were two vehicles with blazing headlights on either side of us. Jock took no notice of them.

It took a while to open the tied-down door bolt, but when the door swung back, there were five vehicles next to the plane – the closest one a panel van of the airport police.

"Happy days are here again, Jock," I said as a hefty man in uniform climbed out of the panel van, settling his cap neatly on his head with elaborate arm movements. "With that rum breath of yours you'll be sleeping in the cells again tonight."

"Not a chance." He'd cut the engines already and the propellers were losing speed. "How many people do we have on board?"

"With you and me, sixty-three."

"It's a mercy they're so thin."

Somebody pushed up some steps and the fat man in uniform was at the top facing us before the steps were properly in place. "Who is the pilot here?"

"I am. Jock Mills is the name." He extended his hand, but the policeman had no desire to make his acquaintance.

"You don't know much about aviation regulations, I gather."

"Give me any page number and I'll recite it for you."

"Come with me, please."

"Where to?"

"I'm asking the questions, Mr Miles. You supply the answers."

"Meet my flight engineer, Mr Brand de la Rey. And my sixty-one passengers."

The man ignored me. And he was fully intending to ignore the passengers as well, but I think the smell got to him. He looked – and looked again. He turned round to get out, and then looked a third time.

"There are still some three hundred waiting in the Ubombo bundu. They're all at last gasp. So, either we're going to try saving their lives or we're going to waste precious time with aviation regulations."

NINE

The longer you had dealings with Jock Mills, the more you realized that he'd always be the right man at the wrong time. In every situation in which he cropped up he would almost immediately become part of the solution and the cause of a new problem. He was a small, inconspicuous man who lived so obstinately by his own rules that he attracted attention everywhere. The longer I knew him, the more difficult I found it to discern the violinist in him. Strydom's theory was simplicity itself. "Make no mistake. He remains a virtuoso, whether with an aeroplane or a violin." With such lack of training and experience and money no other mortal would have got that Dakota's engines running or got the thing into the air – not to mention transporting passengers.

The chief technician at Durban airport, a slender man with delicate fingers and an improbable name like Valentino, said more or less the same. Some four of them were checking the Dakota for a report to civil aviation. He came to join me in the cafeteria with a soggy tomato sandwich and a cup of bluish tea and shook his head. "Your plane is the only one of its kind on earth."

"How come?"

"No part of it works like any part of any other Dakota. The Mills chap fixed everything that was broken in his own way. I don't know how you got that thing into the air. He is either mad or he's a genius."

"Bit of both, I suspect."

Medical personnel were helping the Chopis into a bus one by one. After a while a Dr Bruyns came to introduce himself. He was the superintendent of the Red Cross camp at Umbilo.

"These people are in an abysmal state. Are they the weakest?"

"The strongest. They're the ones who had strength enough to get onto the plane unaided."

"How many are there left?"

"Probably two hundred and fifty."

"It's a long time since I've seen people in such a condition."

"I think whoever decides Mr Mills's fate should take that into consideration. It was an emergency measure."

Mills was allowed to leave after an hour, on condition that he remain in daily contact with the airport authorities, but his plane was confiscated. He said goodbye to nobody; I saw him getting into a taxi and driving away. Dr Bruyns reported after a while that the Red Cross was negotiating with the army to make a cargo plane available to pick up the rest of the refugees.

I could only shake my head. "The mission station has been trying for weeks, but they don't even return their calls."

"I know how it is. But they've got their hands full. You should see what it looks like in the Free State and the Northern Cape. There is so much need among our own people that they can't really afford unnecessary sympathy for foreigners. I think it will help if we show them the state the people are in."

It was just after twelve.

I would have to make a plan to get home again. I was without a cent and the road to Mbabala was not exactly a hitch-hiker's paradise. Dr Bruyns lent me his mobile phone to call Vukile, and he promised to send someone with my bakkie to fetch me – I should stay just where I was.

In the end it wasn't Julia, as I'd expected. She was on night duty and had only got to bed after eleven that morning. Vukile himself was too busy. An ashen and bitterly crabby Jenny came in by the big swing doors at six o'clock that afternoon and without any greeting walked straight past me and disappeared into the cloakroom.

When she emerged ten minutes later, her face had been washed and her hair combed. "Where's Jock?"

"He cleared out. I don't know where to."

"As usual. If he can't be the big hero, he turns tail. Can we go now?"

"You're not hungry by any chance?"

"I haven't eaten since last night, but we must try to get to my car tonight."

"You wouldn't have some money on you, would you?"

"Just enough for petrol."

She wanted to go to Jock's flat first. "Perhaps he can take you back and bring me my car. I was supposed to be back at work today." It was a thatched outhouse in the backyard of a dilapidated old building in Cato Manor. He wasn't there, and judging by the sheaf of accounts protruding from under his door, he hadn't been home for a very long time. "Damn! I don't believe this."

"We can wait for a while if you like."

"That won't be any use. He's got some little bitch that he always scuttles to when things aren't going well with him. That's probably where he is again."

She slept for the first two hundred kilometres.

In Mtubatuba we bought drumsticks and chips from a takeaway. We said only the essential things to each other; I was tired and not in the mood for unnecessary chit-chat, and she very definitely wasn't either. At the Jozini turn-off she offered to drive and when I declined, she curled up and went back to sleep.

It was somewhere on the plains south of the Ubombo that I noticed she was watching me.

"I thought you were asleep."

She just remained sitting motionlessly like that, her legs drawn up, her head against the window, her face expressionless, looking at me.

"What do you see?"

"I wish I knew."

"If you like," I said, "you can drive, then I can look at you."

"I don't care."

I pulled off the road and got out. The night was stuffy and dead quiet. There was lightning very far in the south and I waited for a moment to see whether it would flash up again. I didn't hear her get out, but suddenly her face was right by my elbow. "What are you doing?"

"I thought I saw lightning."

Every time she was close to me, I was aware of the restlessness she carried with her. For the first day or two I didn't know exactly what it was, but that afternoon when she stood in front of me at the airport I realized that she reminded me of the rhebok that Vusi and I had cared for for a while. We kept her in a big cage of jackal wire while she was recovering from a wound in her neck. She hardly ever stood still. Her head, her ears, her skin, her nostrils, something was always in motion – her eyes were always dark and distrustful, piercing past you at something far beyond you. Jenny was exactly like that. Even in the dark, that night, I knew it.

"We can't stand here waiting for the lightning. We've got to get going."

I once again experienced that moment, like the first evening in the shower, of suddenly feeling that I was on the verge of something that wanted to draw me in, and me hesitating, suddenly short of breath, because I knew that it was going to be the beginning of a nightmare.

She turned round and got in behind the wheel of the bakkie. "Come!" The lightning was again intermittently visible, bitterly far beyond the ridge of the plain. I slammed my door with excessive force, but it wasn't altogether my fault, because she'd started moving forward. "It's a pity," she said halfway between third and fourth gear, "but I suppose it's just as well."

"What?"

"You're a bit scared of me."

At one o'clock that morning we stopped in the yard. It was the first time I'd been home since the gale. In the light of the bakkie

I couldn't see much storm damage. The windows were still intact and the doors locked. I lit the lamps. The house was stuffy and dead flies and beetles and praying mantises were strewn all over the place.

"There's no fire under the drum, but the water is lukewarm if you want to shower."

"I will."

I went and lit a candle in the bedroom, opened the window and shook out the blanket to get rid of the worst of the dust and the dead bugs. I could hear Jenny showering outside. To this day I don't know exactly what happened that night. I went and poured myself a brandy and drank it neat and fell asleep on the sofa in the sitting room. I couldn't recall later hearing her come in. The next day, while scratching my head over the incident, I kept feeling like somebody who'd turned up at the theatre only after the first act. I remember she was riding me and leaning over backwards – I couldn't see her face but her breasts were high and triumphant above me against the faint light of the window and I know that at one stage I got hold of the beads around her waist and felt them breaking suddenly and scattering asunder and rolling away in the dark in between the cupboards and chair legs. That morning just after daybreak when I got up, the candle was still burning in the bedroom. She hadn't slept in her bed. The beads were still strewn all over the place and there was a copper bracelet on the kitchen table.

Her car was gone.

2

I'd fallen far behind in my work. Some of the bases that had to be visited daily had not been read in more than a week. Vusi was still at Mbabala, but I decided to drive the rounds first to see what remained of our work after the gale and then to fetch Vusi in the late afternoon.

I had to give it up for a bad job before nine that morning. The previous night on the way home there had been uprooted trees at short intervals, but we'd managed to squeeze past every time. On the narrow bush roads it was more tricky. I was having to stop all the time to hack off branches and drag them away. After the fifth, sixth branch the axe had lost its handle and my hands were full of blisters. Despite three hours of hard labour I'd hardly covered ten kilometres.

I decided to fetch Vusi.

When I arrived, Julia and Vukile were taking turns quibbling with someone on the telephone. Julia stuffed the phone into Vukile's hand when she saw me and signalled me to come with her.

"Who are you bickering with like that?" I demanded.

"The army."

"They don't want to help?"

"They're awaiting orders. Everybody's awaiting orders. They're flying food to the Red Cross camps, so they don't have planes available to send here. This General Somebody now tells us that the Red Cross camps are in any case too full and as far as he knows, we're part of Mozambique."

"But I spoke to a Dr Bruyns in Durban yesterday who promised that he'd arrange with the army to fetch the people."

"I know. He's phoned three times already this morning. They don't want to help him either. You should see what it looks like out there."

"Are there still new ones arriving?"

"Fortunately not that many. Two or three a day. But last night again eleven turned up here."

"It can't carry on like this, Julia."

"De Gaspri is bringing us fifty bags of mealie-meal on Monday."

"Which comes from where?"

"I don't know. Vukile's arranged something with an emergency fund or something in Durban. I just hope we can last till Monday. We're starting to lose more and more people. More by the day. Nine last night. We can't dig graves fast enough."

Vusi and Gwaja and three of the strongest among the refugees were digging a mass grave. I helped them. There was no cloth or canvas or sack in which to wrap the bodies. We stacked them all on top of each other and covered them.

One of them was the woman with the red beads.

3

It took Vusi and me two days to clear the seventy kilometres of bush road on which our experimental stations were situated. Of the nineteen experiments that had still been delivering data before the gale, not a single one remained. It was clear that the wind had not only uprooted trees; it had blown the last bit of moisture out of the soil. Quite a few of our experiments were dependent on a modicum of moisture. The one phenomenon I could not understand was that the control experiments where we'd artificially provided moisture (those few not damaged by the wind) were just as dead and desolate as those dried out by the wind.

More than a year's work had been wiped out completely. The data we'd gathered was not enough to support any conclusions and couldn't be applied unmodified to new experiments.

Vusi and I did not exchange a single word that second day. We chopped and drove and looked and cleared up and each time hoped that perhaps something salvageable had remained at the next station. There was nothing.

At five o'clock the sun clouded over in a red bank on the horizon. We were against the ravines next to the Bápe. We clambered up the near face and for the very first time came across a dead baboon – the emaciated cadaver of a young female hanging from the dry karri branches as if she'd toppled down into them.

We sat waiting for the evening and saw the troop silently climbing up the opposite face. There was something mechanical in their movements. It put me in mind of a rehearsal for some sombre ceremony. The troop was smaller than usual. But after a while we became aware of baboons behind us as well. For the first time since we'd known the Bápe troop, some of them had come to sleep on the eastern face. Most of those on our side of the kloof were females; those on the other side were all males. The females came up to us. Some of them so close that we could see the little crusts of salt in the corners of their eyes. They were restless because they didn't really want us there, but at the same time they were possessive of their little bit of rock face. They were clearly not going to sit aside waiting for us to clear off. They kept moving around us. Five or six of them would sit watching us while the others would circle us apparently aimlessly at a distance; then these would take over the watch and some of the others would mill around us.

There was a strange sound among them which we couldn't quite make out. It was a very soft tapping sound as if one of them was walking with a badly made wooden leg. We watched them more closely to see if we could trace the origin of the sound. After a while Vusi pointed at one of the larger females. She had something in her hand, a scrap of sack or cloth. As long as she could get by on three legs, we couldn't hear her walk – but as soon as she had to use the other front paw and couldn't move the cloth to another foot in time, something inside the cloth – something like a dry wild orange or calabash – struck the rock. Of all of them she was the most restless. Possibly because she'd noticed that we were watching her more and more closely. She lifted her eyebrows and charged me and then jumped round, but in the process lost her cloth. For a second it lay on the hot rock in front of me before she could grab it and take off with it. It was the dry head and scrap of hide and tail of what earlier in the summer would have been her offspring – only the nostrils and eye sockets recognizable in the little skull rattling in the desiccated scalp when she stepped on the wrong front paw. She snatched up the thing frantically from under my gaze and with the scrap of child she sat down at a distance to protest.

We got home only long after dark. Vusi started packing firewood in the fireplace and asked me what I wanted to eat.

"Nothing, thanks."

He was on the point of lighting the scrap of crumpled paper under the kindling. He blew it out and replaced the stove plate. "I am not hungry either."

It was the second night we'd not felt up to eating. The previous night it had been because we couldn't get the smell of death from our hands. We'd carried it with us all day and tried scrubbing it off that afternoon in the yard, but I kept remembering the dead faces from which all hope had departed. All the eyes, except those of the woman with the red beads, were more or less shut; only a little bit of white showed, a bit of dirtyish white like old ivory. Hope was in vain. I kept remembering the dead eyes and the skeletons – because these were not corpses we were burying, they were skeletons. They were so light, I could carry two at a time. And every time when I thought I was clean at last, I would remember the eyes of the woman with the red beads, which we could not get shut. Then I started washing myself all over again and tried to forget all over again.

Vusi was still standing in the kitchen doorway, his shoulder against the jamb. He was looking at the darkness.

"What are we going to do?" he asked after a while, when he noticed I was looking at him.

"I don't know."

"Are we going to start from the beginning?"

"There is nothing left here. Everything is dead."

"No."

"Not? Have you noticed, there aren't even moths around the lamp at night any more?"

"Wait until the rain comes."

"Which is when, Vusi?"

"It will be a long time, but not such a very long time."

I turned up the lamp slightly and walked to the pantry and poured myself a tot of brandy. It was the first time in a very long while that I'd felt up to drinking on my own.

"Show me when you see the clouds."

4

I drew up a report on my doings every month and gave it to de Gaspri to post. Professor Stokes sometimes provided feedback and sometimes not. Now and again there was a copy of the minutes of the Nature Foundation in which I was encouraged and thanked for the work I was doing. But most of the time I had the impression that even Stokes did not know exactly what I was doing or why I was doing it.

There wasn't really any choice. I had to inform Stokes and company that the whole year's work had been lost and that I would understand if they should decide to recall me. All that remained for me was to carry on with my observations of the effects of the drought on the immediate environment. Judging by news from the outside world and by the little I'd seen for myself on the way back from Durban, the effect of the drought until before our gale was smaller in our area than in more populous regions.

I reported in as much detail as necessary on the projects on which I was working, the results I'd obtained and those that I believed to be lost. I gave indications of drought-related phenomena that I was monitoring and that, depending on the duration of the drought, could prove illuminating.

I worked late into the nights, because I wanted to finish the report in time for de Gaspri to post it for me.

That Friday evening just after eleven I'd done with the writing. Vusi had been several times to tell me that supper was on the table, but I wanted to finish first. With the twenty or so typed pages in an envelope and addressed, I took the lamp, locked the door to the outside room and walked down to the house. Vusi was waiting for me in the yard. For a change it wasn't tinned food; it was a spaghetti concoction with what tasted to me like satinflower.

We ate on the back stoep. At least, I ate. He claimed he wasn't hungry, but the little iron pot with cold porridge stood to one side on the stove, and there was no porridge on my plate. He liked scraping out the previous evening's cold porridge in the morning to heat up for breakfast with tomato sauce and chutney. It generally cost me some smooth talk to get a smidgeon of it.

I had just started eating when I heard a distant drone. There was a wild moment in which I was sure it was the rumble of thunder. I could see Vusi lift his head, listening.

"*Iyadumo!*" (The weather is thundery.)

He shook his head.

"No?"

But by that time I could hear it myself. It was a motorbike.

"Vusi? Where is Jock Mills's motorbike? Wasn't the thing here in the yard?"

"We left him at Shabeni. We went there on the bike when we flew." The sound was now clearly that of Mills's Harley Davidson labouring up the kloof somewhere beyond Dumisane's hills. I forgot to eat.

It was a warm night with a three-quarter moon and not a cloud in sight and the bush and the mountainside were a dim, faint powder blue as if everything was made of dust, as if you could brush your hand through the mountain and through the Cape beeches in the yard. We sat listening to him coming round the hills and accelerating on the ridge and braking and accelerating along the approach to the steep incline above the house. The clear evening and the swelling and subsiding of the sound of the motorbike lent Jock Mills and his motorbike a supernatural allure they'd never had before. In my mind he – if it was him – was a sunburnt and bearded, mechanically propelled angel approaching through the dark recesses of the forest and descending at last into our kloof and thundering past above the house and vanishing into the drifting and translucent night towards Mbabala.

"How did he get to Shabeni?" I asked when the sound had died away completely. "If the bike was there, he couldn't have got there by bike."

Vusi said it as if it totally went without saying. "He flew."

The next morning at the crack of dawn we drove to Shabeni. There was no sign of the Dakota. But there were fairly fresh tyre tracks.

"It's the woman with the red car," Vusi said as we inspected the tracks.

"How do you know?"

"The back wheels run this side of the front wheels."

Vukile called me on the radio on Sunday morning. Dr Bruyns of the Umbilo Red Cross camp was on the phone; he was urgently looking for Jock Mills. "Do you know where to get hold of him, brother?"

"No."

"Damn!"

"Why? What does he want with Jock?"

"Julia tells me you are coming over today. Maybe we can phone Dr Bruyns while you're here and you can speak to him yourself."

"It will only be by late afternoon. Towards five or six."

"Looking forward, brother. See you then."

I reached the clinic just before five. Vukile and Julia were nowhere to be seen and I walked up the backyard in the direction of the church. There were people everywhere about me, but I didn't want to see them. I was later to recall many things from that time that I hadn't seen while they were happening around me. Because you see so much that you'd rather not see, you become blinded to it. To the bloody ulcers on the legs and the distended bellies and the yearning eyes and pus and swarming blowflies. And later, sometimes years later, when the uncertainty and anguish with which you'd observed everything have at last abated, your memory starts filling in large hiatuses, fraction by fraction, and you remember the child with the little feathers, and suddenly one morning you remember Nandi, who was standing, that first time, on the bare patch next to the clinic swaying as if she was dancing, until you realized that she hadn't danced for a long time, that she was only trying to keep her balance. Later Julia was convinced that Nandi could hear music that nobody else could hear, because she swayed without cease, all the time. Even the morning on which she at last died – on the same lumpy mattress on which I'd tried to sleep that night behind Vukile's desk – even then she lay keeping time with her head and later only with her eyelids to some inaudible *isitolotolo* tune from some summer from a lost, unchronicled youth.

Vukile came to meet me. I could see he was all in. Only that morning there had been three people to bury who'd not shown any symptoms of disease the previous day. "The problem, brother," he explained as we walked to his office, "is that they arrive here so totally famished and weak, even a bout of flu can be fatal."

We phoned Bruyns. He came straight to the point. He had to trace Jock Mills no later than today.

I was cautious. "I hope he's not in trouble again."

"Do you have any contact with him?"

"No."

"Do you have a telephone number or an address?"

"I don't remember the name of the street or the building, but I can try to explain to you. What's he done wrong this time?"

"He has to fly out those people with you for me."

"Using what as an aeroplane?"

"His Dakota."

"It's not his Dakota, it belongs to the army and it's been confiscated. And besides, it's a death trap on wings."

"There's nothing wrong with the plane. I saw the inspection report myself. Apparently the thing is unique; so nobody knows how to fly it. But mechanically it's in good shape."

"I flew in the thing myself, Doctor. We couldn't get altitude."

"You landed safely, and that's all that counts."

"If Mills ever landed at Durban airport again, they'd lock him up."

"I know. That's what they say too. But we've been sitting here all the time right next to a little aerodrome that we didn't know about. It's a bit neglected, but it's usable. He can land here."

"And how does he get his Dakota back from the airport authorities?"

"We steal it."

"You can't be serious, Doctor."

"Why not? I'm absolutely serious. We're talking here about more than two hundred people who are dying of diseases of neglect and hunger. In such circumstances I steal if I have to, and I lie and cheat when I have no choice. You can't expect me to sit and wait for happy days."

"I hear what you're saying, Doctor. But we must be careful that things don't start running away with us. Mills is fairly impulsive and unpredictable, and I don't know if such a person must..."

"Must be what? Thank Heaven for such people. I'm tired of struggling with bureaucratic red tape. We have too many people on this earth who try to be practical all the time at any price."

"But I've always thought the army—"

"They've been keeping me dangling from a string for five days. They don't have aircraft. And they swear high and low that the mission station is over the border."

"What about a private aircraft?"

"The private aircraft help where they can, but they're booked up weeks in advance."

I produced my trump card. "Doctor, I think we must look for another pilot. Mills has a serious drinking problem."

"We have only one aircraft at our disposal, and only one pilot who can fly the thing."

"He drinks a bottle of rum at a time. And he does it on the sly."

But Bruyns was unimpressed. "Leave that to me. We only need him for five or six flights. I'll monitor him."

I directed him as best I could to the place where Jenny Grobler had gone looking for Jock that evening. The chances were slim in any case that he would find him there. And should he find him, the chances were even slimmer that they'd be able to steal a Dakota from the hangars at Durban airport and take off in it without getting caught.

Or that's what I thought.

5

Sister Roma and Sister Erdmann were both out of sorts, and I spent the rest of the day helping Julia and Vukile in the clinic. There was a child with what seemed to be a broken arm and I tried to devise a splint. I sterilized syringes and carried wet mattresses out into the sun and helped to make beds and fed weak patients. I tried to steer clear of the smaller ward with the seriously ill patients. The sounds emanating from there, the incessant sighing and groaning and smothered outcries, were bad enough. But I could hear Julia and Vukile talking. There was a young girl whose pulse Vukile could no longer detect. Julia held a pocket mirror in front of her mouth. "There *is* still a bit of vapour, Vukile," I heard her say repeatedly. "There's a bit. Look. She's still alive."

"No pulse. Absolutely no pulse."

Things had changed radically since the first refugees had started arriving at the clinic. In the beginning there were blankets and clean linen; the walls and floors shone with cleanliness; all the patients were washed early every morning; Julia was always in a white uniform; Vukile's shirt, admittedly, was usually untucked, but he too was particular about his white pants and shirt and spotless white shoes.

This was no longer so.

Julia came to help feed the people on the stoep. Some could take in only the thin, watery mealie-meal porridge, others crumbled bread soaked in powdered milk or thin gruel with meat extract. One of them was the sparrow child. He was already too weak to feed himself and she picked him up on her lap three times a day and patiently fed him crumb by crumb.

She didn't want me to feed the little ones. According to her I was too clumsy with them. "Slow down, Brand," she cautioned constantly.

"You're feeding too fast. He's going to choke." But I was in a hurry to meet the mouth anxiously and tremblingly and brokenly trying to reach for another teaspoon of food – a young man, perhaps not yet twenty, but decrepit, a small and bony crow lying with his two claws scrabbling in the air and his beak splayed open for a crust of bread. I gazed fascinated at the Adam's apple bobbing restlessly, the near-visible ribcage dilating and contracting around the lungs, the eyes rolling searchingly in their sockets, the tongue lying hesitantly on the lower lip like some little amphibian creature that had hibernated too long in darkness.

At two o'clock Gwaja fetched the young girl to bury her.

I started to learn, the deeper we ventured into the afternoon, about the totally defenceless fragility of skin and bone, about the puniness of everything, about the tiny vapour between everybody and death.

At five o'clock Sister Erdmann came to say she was feeling better; she'd take over for a few hours.

Julia and I were standing washing our hands and faces in a basin in front of her back door. I stood watching our hands and our arms while we were washing; I saw her bare shoulders and her neck, the tongue brushing the lips, and realized that under Julia's tanned skin, under all the youthful softness and unblemishedness, there was a pale white skeleton washing along, participating invisibly, a skeleton preparing itself slowly but surely for the day when it could cast off the winding sheet to show its true face.

"What's the matter, Brand?" she asked after a while, because I hadn't noticed that she was watching me.

"Why?"

"What are you looking at me so oddly for?"

"I didn't know we were like that."

"Like what?"

"This poor…" I couldn't find a word for the little flock that above us in the three stuffy little wards was lying waiting for the night. They were no longer people; they weren't just matter either; they were not dead yet and no longer really living. "These poor… wretches." That was all word I could find. "We look just like them. We just hide it."

"I know."

I picked up the towel and handed it to her.

"I know, Brand. There is nothing we can do about it."

"Except to try to make it as meaningful as possible."

"That's what I'm doing. That's why I'm here."

She opened up the towel and started drying my arms and face.

"I'm no longer sure just why I'm here."

"I understand why you say that. But it will change."

"The whole of last year's work is gone. The little bit that was left was buggered up by the storm."

"I was afraid of that."

"I think they're going to have to cancel my contract. There's no work for me here any more. Except to count skeletons."

"I hope that's not true."

"I just somehow realized this afternoon while I was trying to help feed those people – time is passing us by. Me and you and all of us here."

"Yes. Nowadays I realize that every day. And the more I realize it, the more I try to mean something for these people."

I took the towel from her and dried her face and arms. "To tell you the absolute truth, I can't really imagine life without you, Julia."

"You'll never go away from here."

"Why not?"

"Because you need a place to hide. Just like Vukile and de Gaspri. And Strydom."

"And you?"

"And me. I never want to be anywhere else again. But I must admit, it won't be quite the same place without you."

I put the towel around the back of her neck and pulled her head closer with it till her face was almost up against mine, and she stood looking at me as if conceding that unexpectedly we had arrived at a moment that might make a difference. I kissed her and she didn't avert her face. The towel was still in my hands. I held her face in the towel and kissed her again and again and she didn't mind. I could feel, gradually, her mouth opening under mine. She removed the towel from between us and threw it aside and took me into the house. It was dusk outside and in the room it was almost dark. We took off each other's clothes as if we'd done it many times before. Our hands found their way to every lace and button and loop without casting about blindly in the dark. I don't think she forgot; I know that not for a moment that night did I forget the searching hands and hungry mouths thirty metres from our open window. She fed my body with the same undivided attention and dedication and just as carefully and gently as she'd fed that afternoon's mouths. We made love as one would make love while death was seated somewhere in the house at a game of cards.

I remember once when I went to fetch a drink of water from the bathroom, looking out of the window and seeing Vukile and Sister Erdmann crouching by a bed, each with a lantern next to the face. I could see, every now and again, the little mirror flashing and flashing and flashing in their hands.

TEN

I

The next few days passed at a painfully slow pace for me. There was more than enough work for me, but my mind was constantly absent. I was in bed early every night, but had to lie for hours waiting for sleep to come.

For me the whole world was filled with Julia.

The third evening before we turned in, Vusi asked if something was the matter.

"No, Vusi? Why?"

For a while he sat gazing into the darkness. "Some birds fly away," he said, "because that's how their kind is made; but they come back again, because that's also how they're made."

"You like talking in riddles always. Why do you say so?"

I should have known better. He got up and went and locked himself in his bedroom.

Later I understood slightly more. But also not altogether. Because I was inclined, in time, to think that there was not only a prediction locked up in his words, perhaps there was also a promise.

At first I thought it was Jock Mills hammering at my window that night. It was, after all, halfway between midnight and daybreak, and he was the only person I knew who kept such odd hours. But it was Strydom's voice calling my name from somewhere in the darkness. "De la Rey!" And even before I could reply again, but more loudly: "De la Rey!"

"Strydom, is that you?"

I realized then that it was the first time in the years we'd known each other that he'd given me a name and that I'd called him by his.

"I'm sorry to be a nuisance." In the faint light of my battered torch I could see the reflection of the crack in his spectacle lens. "I was wondering if you perhaps had pills for fever."

"Come round the back."

I went and unlocked the door and lit a lamp and went out. He wasn't by the back door; he was still where I'd left him, talking to somebody.

"Is there somebody with you?" I asked when I got to him.

"Not as far as I know."

"Who are you talking to?"

"I thought I was talking to you."

"Let's go in." I could see he was swaying slightly and when he tried to walk it was clear that he was very unsteady on his feet. I helped him into the kitchen and up to a chair, all the time not sure whether he was seriously ill or had perhaps taken to drink. He didn't smell of drink. And with the lamp burning more brightly, I could see that he was sweating and was very pale.

"What do you think is wrong with you?"

"I don't know. It's been like this for a week." He was short of breath.

"I realized tonight." It was as if he had to pause halfway through every sentence to catch his breath. "I had to get to somebody."

There wasn't very much in my medicine chest. Painkillers and plasters in the wardrobe, snakebite serum in the fridge and brandy on the pantry shelf. That was all.

I made him swallow a handful of painkillers and made up a bed on the sofa. When he was lying down, I gave him a big tablespoon of neat brandy. Within a few minutes he was calmer. But every time just as I thought he was asleep, he suddenly started shaking and saying he was cold.

There was no other way out: I had to get him to Vukile. Just after daybreak I woke up Vusi and brought the bakkie round to the back door so long. But when we tried to carry him out, he protested at the top of his voice. "No, let go. Let me go. I'm not going anywhere."

"We have to get you to a doctor. You need medicine."

"Which doctor?"

"Dr Khumalo at the clinic."

"Absolutely not."

"Why not?"

"That man's doctoring kills everybody. Give me some more of the stuff that you gave me last night. It helps."

When at last I got hold of Vukile by radio and described the symptoms to him, his reaction lent some credence to Strydom's distrust.

"Your guess is as good as mine, brother."

"I administered painkillers and brandy."

"Well done! Stick to that. It might just help to break the fever."

At six o'clock Strydom got a stiff tot of brandy and three pills. He started sweating more and more and complained all the time of the cold. At ten o'clock we gave him the same medicine. It was more or less then that he started getting delirious.

I went into the room and heard him speaking Afrikaans to Vusi. Then I knew he didn't know where he was. Vusi signalled that the man was muddled.

"How are you, Strydom?" It was odd seeing him without his glasses. The glasses were lying on the window sill where Vusi must have put them, and Strydom was looking for me through two myopic eyes as if struggling to see past the cracks in his lenses.

"Have you come to tell me?"

"Tell you what?"

"Even if it's only a piece of the jawbone. They'll come and tell you."

"Who, Strydom?"

He lay looking at the ceiling as if trying to remember who. The shakes were better, but he was still sweating profusely. "They have easy answers. But they could be wrong. So where do the Khoi and the San fit in? Where were they all the time?"

Throughout the morning he wanted to know every so often whether somebody had come to tell yet. Later I ignored it. But that afternoon, while I was feeding him soup, he suddenly turned his head away, as if listening. "Perhaps that's them now."

"Who?"

He tried again to focus his eyes on me. "If it hadn't been for Helena. Just one damned mistake. And just look!"

I sat waiting. I was too scared to ask anything.

"Thirty years of wandering after nothing. Just because of Helena."

He didn't want to eat anything more.

"It's not always easy. You know. In the bush like that. A dither a bother. One cave after the other. Here a little hand bone. There a tooth. In ten years. A bit of vertebra. You know the answer is right there. In front of you in the stone. You don't get it read."

He was hunting anklebones and pelvic bones and hand bones all afternoon. And there was something about the Rift Valley on which he got stuck every time; he was trying to remember something about the Rift Valley. That evening just before sundown Malume and his troop were close to the yard again. We could hear them all the time on the ridge behind the house. There was a grumpiness, a restlessness among them that issued every now and again in a snarling and snapping. I went to shower and I was still drying myself when I heard Strydom shouting. Vusi and I reached him at the same time. He was gesticulating at the window as if trying to ward off something. The window wasn't very big, but big enough to contain Malume's whole body. He was sitting on the window sill as I'd often see him sitting on his ledge on the rock face across the Bápe looking at me. Quite motionless. As if he didn't see me at all and saw everything about me; as if he was staring through my incidental presence at something behind me that he was wondering about. But this time his attention was wholly on Strydom. Vusi slowly moved in between Strydom and the window, careful not to cause further pandemonium. Strydom couldn't utter a word. He just pointed feebly, as if afraid that we couldn't see what he saw.

It was only when Vusi was a single pace from Malume that the animal was prepared to shift his gaze from Strydom to Vusi. But just for a moment. Then he was gone.

It was stuffy, but we closed the window, and gave Strydom a stiff tot of brandy and hoped for the best.

He slept almost immediately. And when he woke up an hour later, it was as if he was a bit more clear-headed. He asked for his spectacles. And when these were placed on his nose and he could see me at last through the cracks, he beckoned me closer, and still closer. "The search is the thing," he whispered confidentially. "The search is the thing. That's all very well. But what does one say about me and Helena?"

I didn't know whether to respond to this. I was scared of saying the wrong thing and thus inhibiting him. But at the same time I was scared that if I said nothing, he might think I wasn't interested. It gradually became clear that he wasn't really talking to anyone other than himself. "She took my life away."

He would say something and then just sit staring in front of him for a few minutes.

"She's written all over everything. Every day. Every night she's around here somewhere. Just standing there. We don't talk. What's really left to say?"

Now and again it was as if he became aware of me again. But then he'd forget again and re-enter his own world.

"If I draw water from the pools. The crickets in the grass. The one stray raindrop falling on me at night when I'm sitting by the fire. It's all her, I suppose." Strydom suddenly tried to get to his feet. As if something had occurred to him. Something that he urgently had to go and do.

"Strydom, wait. Sit. Where are you going?"

"One Godalmighty tiny little misunderstanding. And everything comes to naught. As if a fatal fault line in the earth's crust had been waiting just for that." I persuaded him at length to lie down and turned down the lamp. He didn't want to take off his glasses.

"On the other hand, what do you do? Pick up pebbles. Frighten the bats. Chip away at the floors and walls where no water has dripped. Measure and fit and join. Look for a bit of a molar. Perhaps later one will understand something."

He went to sleep while he was talking, and woke up only once that night, some time after eleven, when I'd gone to bed already. "De la Rey, are you here?" I heard him ask.

"In my room."

"I dreamt I saw him. But completely. Everything. He's sitting here in the window."

"Yes, Strydom."

I woke up in the early hours to the sound of Mills's motorbike coming up the kloof and disappearing slowly and tortuously over the hills towards Shabeni.

2

Bruyns sat by the fire that evening telling me about his search for Jock Mills. There was nothing to eat, but we made a fire for a bit of light. There was no moon and neither of our torches was up to much. We came across a dry thorn tree that had been uprooted by the storm. There was a hollow in the ground where the roots had been torn out. With the thinner branches, I devised a fire in the hollow between the thick roots and we sat watching the flames patiently licking and nibbling at the roots until at last the whole trunk was alight.

Bruyns was not a man for detail. He supplied only the most essential facts; the rest I had to ask him for.

Mills was, as everybody could have predicted, not at his sleeping quarters when Bruyns went to look for him. Not the first evening; nor the following morning or the second evening. Bruyns left a note under his door and messages with all the neighbours. He phoned Red Cross headquarters in Johannesburg three times a day to ask whether they'd managed to get hold of another plane yet. At the same time he started negotiating with the airport authorities for permission to retrieve the Dakota. For a variety of reasons they weren't even prepared to listen to him. In the first place the Dakota was army property; the army had been informed and any day now they'd come and remove the plane, even if it should mean they had to disassemble it and transport it by road. In the second place civil aviation had launched an inquiry against Mills because he hadn't submitted a flight plan beforehand, had landed without permission at a public airport, ignored landing instructions, apparently wasn't in possession of a valid flying licence and had illegally appropriated army property. In the third place they'd decided that the Dakota was not safe to transport passengers.

Bruyns talked an old soldier friend into negotiating on his behalf with the army in Pretoria. Perhaps they would, once they'd been made aware under what circumstances Mills had "appropriated" the plane, reconsider the matter.

On the third day Mills had phoned him and they'd met each other at the Red Cross camp. Bruyns asked him if he was prepared to transport the rest of the refugees at Mbabala with the confiscated plane. It was a superfluous question. He was more than prepared. Even if they had to steal the plane. He was in fact still constantly plotting how to reclaim her. In his eyes this wouldn't really consti- tute theft – the plane had been rusting away in the veld for years and he'd been spending all his bread money for long enough on fixing her up.

Bruyns went to show him the airstrip behind the Red Cross camp. It was about fifty metres too short, but they could extend it without much trouble.

Petrol was a problem. Because although Mills had a few thousand litres of petrol at his disposal at Shabeni, and although he had ac- cording to his calculations siphoned in enough for a return flight, the Dakota had used more fuel than anticipated on the way to Durban. There was a possibility that they might not reach Shabeni.

Bruyns's fishing vehicle was a totally rust-riddled 4×4 with a corroded exhaust system. The thing was strong enough to haul the Dakota from the hangar, but then they'd have to muffle the engine. With the aid of a few hundred rand from Bruyns's pocket Mills had fitted a new silencer and bought four twenty-five-litre canisters of fuel.

They didn't want to inform the people at Mbabala of their plans before they were sure they could successfully remove the plane from the airport.

Whatever they wanted to do, they'd have to do at night, and at night all the hangars were locked; it would in any case be extremely tricky for an inexperienced pilot like Mills to take off at night. By day there were too many people and too much other air traffic. There was no moon – they'd be able to cut the security fences behind the hangars and tow the plane unnoticed from the airport area by a side street. But they abandoned this plan almost immediately, because the fence was probably electrified and it would be well-nigh impossible to tow the Dakota by road for several kilometres to the Red Cross airstrip.

Because Bruyns was in the employ of the Red Cross and often flew light aircraft all over Natal, he knew two or three airport officials. One of these was Brian Symcox, manager of the airport cafeteria. Symcox knew more or less everybody at the airport – including the chief of security and the control-tower personnel.

It was easy to establish that the control tower never shut down, but that between 24.00 and 04.30 there was only one operator on call for emergencies. It was just as easy to find out where the Dakota was kept and where the keys to the hangars were kept. Mills's plane was in hangar number five and the keys were locked in the airport strongroom every evening at six. Hangar five's two keys were on their own ring on the main bunch and this bunch was kept in the grounds supervisor's steel cabinet during the day. The nearest locksmith was a twenty-minute drive from the airport. The supervisor was rarely in his office in the mornings and the cabinet was never locked. But he locked his office even when he went to the toilet and the office key was on a chain attached to his belt.

That afternoon they'd known they had to reach a decision. Either they had to wait until some plane or other became available, which could happen when it was much too late, or they had to go and retrieve Mills's DC-3.

The decision had taken itself.

The Red Cross office reported that the situation was becoming desperate. Cholera had broken out in the Eastern Cape and in the Vaal Triangle, and the chances of helping the Mbabala people were consequently that much slimmer.

At four o'clock on the dot that afternoon Jock Mills had a serious heart attack ten metres from the office door of the supervisor. Three people rushed to his aid immediately. One of them was the supervisor. Three minutes later a doctor appeared on the scene, a Dr Antonie Bruyns, who had been in the building by chance. Bruyns asked the supervisor to keep the patient upright in a seated position while he went to phone to arrange for an ambulance. That was enough time to impress the profile of hangar five's keys onto a tin of putty. The Red Cross ambulance came to pick up Mills. At five o'clock Bruyns came to thank the supervisor for his help with the heart patient. The patient was in hospital and out of danger. At seven o'clock, when Brian Symcox drove home in his panel van, he closed the service gate next to the kitchens behind him, hooking in the padlock but not locking it.

At quarter-past three the next morning Bruyns and Mills had driven in by the same gate, unlocked hangar five, towed the Dakota to the farthest runway with the 4×4 and started the engines. When he was certain Mills was ready, Bruyns drove back slowly to the service gate, locked it from the outside, and drove out to the main road. At the Tammy's Bar turn-off he stopped, switched off the engine and waited. At thirteen minutes past four Mills's DC-3 passed over him and swerved south. He'd have to stay aloft till after daybreak, because in the dark he'd never be able to see the Red Cross airstrip or make a landing there.

He touched down just before five. They poured in the four cans of petrol and Mills spent the rest of the day checking the plane.

They couldn't fly straight to Mbabala, because they'd first have to go and pick up petrol at Shabeni. Then, late in the afternoon, they went to phone Vukile Khumalo to ask that somebody should be waiting for them at Shabeni in case something went awry with the landing. The only somebody in the vicinity was me. They wanted to fill the tanks that night and fly two consignments of refugees to Umbilo the next morning.

I was at the airstrip an hour before sundown. Mills landed just before dark. Not a bad landing for a pilot and a plane that had both been weighed officially and found wanting. This time I had a proper ladder with me that I could prop up in front of the door. When the door opened at last, Bruyns stood there looking down at me. I could see he wasn't well. He was as pale as wax. Mills appeared a bit later. He too looked fairly battered and in a bad mood.

"His problem," Bruyns explained a few days later, "is lack of sleep, a few days' serious alcohol abuse, and most probably a mild case of depression." Mills was fast asleep by that time, curled up like a millipede on his bit of sponge mattress in the back of the plane. "But a few hours of good sleep will improve matters."

"You're sure he hasn't got liquor on him?"

"Convinced. Unless he's nailed it down somewhere in a wing."

"That's not impossible."

"We'll know first thing tomorrow morning."

3

Mills was very sober the next morning. "Have you ever seen such a beautiful day?" he asked exuberantly when just after sunrise I emerged from my bakkie, where I'd been trying to get some sleep on the sagging seat. I looked around, saw only a stretch of barren veld and shook my head.

"Where's the doctor?" Mills always referred respectfully to Bruyns as "the doctor". In his eyes "the doctor" had retrieved him from the edge of a complete breakdown and convinced him that in spite of everything the world had a real need of him.

"He's gone for a walk. I think he's a worried man."

"Why?"

"He didn't know a Dakota could bump like that."

"You'll have to get a move on, you two. As I know Julia, her passengers have been lined up and waiting since dawn."

Bruyns did his best to hide it, but it was clear, when he showed up after a while, that he was far from easy in his mind.

The engines took with ease. I could see Bruyns crossing himself just before closing the door. He may well have tried telling somebody else he was just joking, but I was close enough to see that he was fervently praying.

They took off with the sun, and apparently just as effortlessly.

That day I carted two bakkie-loads of petrol drums from Shabeni to Mbabala. On the way back to collect another load I turned off to my house to check on Strydom. He was still weak, but he could feed himself and walk a few steps at a time. Whatever had been ailing him, a whole bottle of brandy and two packets of painkillers later he was on the mend. I found him on the back stoep, indignantly awaiting my arrival.

"Have you got my truck's key?"

"Why?"

"Vusi can't find it anywhere. And it's not in the truck either."

"You're surely not thinking of driving."

"I should be OK by tomorrow."

"Strydom, if you drive off before I'm back, you needn't come back. Because then you're an obstreperous no-good and I have no time for such people."

"How am I supposed to drive without my key?"

I fetched the key from the pantry shelf and gave it to him. And drove off.

On that stretch of road with its kloofs and mountains listening to the radio is a lost cause. I nevertheless tried that day, more from boredom than anything else, to see if I could pick up a voice or a scrap of music. In between the constant crackling and scratching I could hear something now and again. In the snippets of one o'clock news that I could make out there was, apart from lots of references to cholera and emergency aid and the country's dams that were on average four per cent full, also mention of the... aircraft that... and of which, in spite of... no trace has been found since... last night briefly on the radar screens...

It almost sounded as if it could be Mills's Dakota that they were talking about.

I had hoped, when I was unloading the first consignment of petrol, that there would be news of Mills and Bruyns. But they hadn't returned. Julia and her helpers were carrying the weakest of the remaining patients one by one and installing them in the shade of a rickety shelter that Gwaja had devised from laths and palm fronds. When long after dark I stopped next to the airstrip with the last consignment, there was still no plane. There were a few lanterns under the shelter and by their faint light I could see Julia pottering about amidst her little gathering of people.

"What are you still doing here?" I asked as I pulled up next to her.

"We're waiting for better days."

"Mills and Bruyns not turned up yet?"

"No." She leant down and kissed my cheek through the open window. "They're having problems." Her voice was worn out.

"What's it this time?"

"The whole country is looking for them."

"They haven't gone missing, have they?"

"Everybody thinks so. But we know where they are."

Apparently there had been news reports all day about the "army plane" that had "inexplicably disappeared" from the airport's hangars "in broad daylight".

Bruyns had phoned that afternoon to say that they'd landed safely in Umbilo, but that it would be too risky to take off again immediately. Durban airport was frantically scanning its radar screens for an unscheduled flight. The only reason they'd been able on that morning's flight to fly unnoticed for about ninety-nine per cent of the time was that the Dakota could once again not gain altitude and had flown so low that the radar couldn't pick it up. Their plan was to take off again the next morning at two o'clock. Mbabala's airstrip had to be illuminated with two large fires at the two farthest points. They could then land another consignment of people at Umbilo before daybreak.

"I don't know if it's a good thing, Julia. Even in broad daylight Jock and that Dakota are not a good combination."

"It's that or nothing."

Afterwards I often thought that we were all probably a bit mad at that time. We were embarked on an absurd operation that under any circumstances would have been classified as irresponsible and even reckless. But in time circumstances diminished our choices one by one. We were in a place where totally unacceptable ways out had become the only ways out.

At the farthest point of the airstrip Gwaja's first fire was leaping up higher and higher into the darkness. The process had been set in motion, and the only way to stop it would be to come up with a better plan.

"How many people are left?"

"Hundred and eighty something. That's three loads. I'd so hoped they could do two flights per day."

"Are there no new people turning up?"

"None for more than a week now. We're now losing more than we gain."

I went to help Gwaja stoke the fires up further.

It was not a problem for these people to sleep in the open. In their long journey south from Mozambique and in their time at Mbabala, most of them had had to sleep in the open anyway. It didn't get cold at night and of rain there was under the circumstances no prospect. It was too much of a hullabaloo to schlep everybody back to the clinic. They made a smaller fire near the shelter and Sister Roma and her helpers brought food and helped everybody to find a place to sleep.

With the fires going, the petrol unloaded and everybody fed and more or less quiet, at least six hours of waiting remained. It was Sister Erdmann's turn for night duty, but she couldn't help the people at the clinic and those next to the airstrip at the same time. Sister Roma volunteered to help at the airstrip so that Julia could get some sleep.

We walked back to the clinic.

It was the first time that we could be together since the previous Sunday night.

She took my hand in hers and we followed my torch's faint dot of light into the darkness. "Why did I miss you more this week than before?" she demanded.

"So you did miss me before?"

"That would seem to be the implication, wouldn't it?"

"Then we've been wasting a lot of time, Julia Krige."

"No."

"No? You've known for a long time how I feel about you."

"My head wasn't quite right for it. The circumstances weren't right. The circumstances are still not right."

"But your head is better."

"Yes."

We were in front of her back door. There where everything had started that Sunday afternoon. She unlocked the door and we went in and without lighting the lamps we first opened all the windows and the front door, because the house was stuffy. At the last window she came and stood next to me and I held her.

"It's been a hellishly long week, Julia. I felt all the time as if there were a huge black vacuum here where you are now."

"And so there was." I kissed her hands. "Perhaps it's not the right thing we're doing. I don't know. But I don't want to stop it, Brand. I can't any more. I just want you over and over again."

It felt, from when we'd arrived at the back door until much later when we lay talking in each other's arms, spent and contented, as if it was the very first time. Because it was like a first time. Each time that night it was like another first time. We explored and experienced each other anew time after time as if we'd never done it before.

Just before twelve we were back at the airstrip.

There were more than sixty people under the shelter, and although they were all awake by now, nobody spoke. We were waiting for the Dakota. There was lightning in the north, where we hadn't seen lightning for a very long time. And the evening was unusually quiet. But at that time you could say that every night. We were all used to many night sounds. Crickets there always were. And frogs. And night birds. But all that summer the nights had been dead quiet. Without wind, without birds, without jackals. At times you could hear yourself breathe.

We heard the Dakota approach from very far away. The Chopis long before us. They started talking among themselves, and it was only when we noticed that that we could hear it – an even drone like a rising wind. Gwaja's fires were big and bright and I went to switch on the bakkie lights. We could eventually hear by the sound that the plane was near, but we could see nothing. It was only after it had landed and was close to us that we could make out the high back against the night sky, thundering towards us.

Mills hardly greeted anybody when he got out. He indicated something to Bruyns and disappeared into the darkness.

"His stomach is upset. If you're asking me, his nerves are giving him hell."

I was surprised to see Bruyns on the plane. I'd been sure that he'd send somebody else in his place this time. He helped me draw petrol while Julia and the others helped the people up the ladder one by one. Bruyns was quieter than usual. He was visibly tired and tense.

"How many plane loads after this one?" he asked.

"Two more. Perhaps three."

"It's just a question of time before they lock us up. I suspect they've found out where we land. All they had to do was figure out which airstrip was closest to the Red Cross camp."

"But you're in charge of the camp, after all. They have no jurisdiction there."

"The airstrip isn't part of the camp. And in any case the army does just as it likes. Ask me, I know."

"They won't do anything. They know you're trying to help."

"That's what I thought the first time."

"And then?"

"Then they stripped me of my rank and stuffed me in the hole for three weeks." There were no detention barracks and transgressors like him were shut up in a hole in the ground.

"When was that?"

"In Angola. Because I tried to help one of the Cubans. His arm had been shot off and he was bleeding to death. If we arrive at Umbilo tonight and they're waiting for us, it's the end of this lot left here."

Mills was suddenly with us again. "They won't get me. Not alive."

"What are you saying, Jock!"

"I've often thought it must be a nice way to die. You fly to hell and gone. You literally fly to kingdom come."

"Sounds as if your stomach is still giving you trouble."

"You sit in that machine and the world is your oyster. You see for 180 degrees. You just keep on flying. The petrol won't run out in both tanks simultaneously. First one engine will cut out. Then you know it's getting close. Then the other one cuts. And it's dead quiet. You hear nothing. You float like a bird. It must be the most wonderful feeling. Nobody can get close to you. You're free. Nobody can touch you. You sit for one last time looking at everything. At the earth coming closer and closer. Till the trees are level with your feet. Then you close your eyes. It will be very fast. Very fast. I don't think you'll feel anything."

We pretended not to hear him and that seemed to suit him. They took off just after three.

There were two, at most three, loads of people left, but the weakest had at last been taken off our hands.

4

Strydom was still there when I got home the next morning. Grumpy and full of gripes and shaky, but clearly not ill any more. Vusi was just as sulky. Neither of them wanted to say what the matter was, but I gathered that they'd had their differences. Vusi could speak neither Afrikaans nor English, and Strydom couldn't speak Zulu; the few words that he did know, he generally used incorrectly, which had in the past led to unnecessary misunderstanding.

The month's provisions were delivered halfway through the morning, and it was remarkable how immediately this changed the mood of both of them.

I invited de Gaspri in for coffee, but as usual he was in a hurry. We stood talking next to his old rattletrap of a two-tonner with its cross-eyed headlights and the smoking exhaust, while his assistant and Vusi unloaded the usual: a drum of diesel, a bag of coal, paraffin, mealie-meal, canned food, pasta – all the normal things. The little packet of post was just a few newsletters and technical journals. There was nothing from head office.

"If it carries on like this," de Gaspri was saying, "then the rain may be here soon."

"Why do you say that?"

"With the rain in Mozambique."

"It's been raining in Mozambique?"

"Good rains. From Maputo to the north. And in Swaziland. Starting yesterday."

I hadn't thought I would ever again hear somebody talk of good rains. You start accepting, in time, that the drought is here to stay, that it won't change easily – in any case not without a miracle.

"Vusi," I said when de Gaspri had left, "I hear stories of rain."

"That's what I said, that it won't be long now. A little bit long, but not very long."

"How long, Vusi?"

"*Masinyane*" was the word he used, that can probably be translated as "within a reasonable time". A vague word that could just as well mean "tomorrow" as "in a month's time".

That evening while Strydom and I were sitting on the front stoep waiting for supper, I told him about the rain in Mozambique.

"Then I am right, after all," he said. "My joints have been aching for two days. But I thought it was because of the stupid fever that I was so full of aches and pains." I suddenly realized that while he'd been delirious he hadn't used the word "stupid" once. "It's March. It's late for rain. But it's possible. I suppose you'll be glad."

"Won't you?"

"What difference does it make to me?"

A few bottles of wine had arrived with the provisions and I went to fetch one from the fridge.

"You won't mind, then, if I get going again tomorrow?" he asked as I returned with the bottle and two glasses.

"If you think you've recovered."

The baboons were on the ridge next to the house again. We could hear them carping and snarling at one another every now and again. Strydom's eyes kept wandering in that direction, as if wanting to make sure that we wouldn't be caught unawares again.

"I want to say thank you," he said, "that you took me in. I wouldn't have made it on my own. And I also want to say," he added before I could even respond, "that if perhaps I talked a load of shit – just forget it. It was the fever talking."

Suddenly evening descended on the yard – an expected visitor, but one that had arrived too early. I poured Strydom a glass of wine. He took the glass from me, first glanced at the ridge where it was now almost dark, then aimed in my direction past the crack in his lens until he had me full in his sights, and lifted his glass. "So."

ELEVEN

I

Julia called me by radio somewhere in the early hours to say that it was long after three and Mills had not turned up yet. I was digging around in my sleep-befuddled brain for practical explanations – there were many, I just couldn't think of them all fast enough – when she asked me if we were also having lightning. I was going to say no, not as far as I knew, when the window in front of me turned into a blue block of light in which I saw the yard and the trees and the mountains across the way flickering for a moment and then disappearing. The radio was suddenly just a roar. I tried to call her again from my side, but the roar was only worse. Then it flickered again. And again.

I went out onto the back stoep because the lightning was somewhere behind us in the north, far behind Dumisane's hills. I went and stood in the yard watching the light flash up from behind the high ridge of the mountain, first intermittently and then almost continuously, brighter and brighter; without thunder, without wind – like an old movie without sound making unrecognizable images dance on a dark screen.

I don't know when Vusi emerged from his room. He could have been there before me. I saw him at some distance to the left of me on a bare patch, watching. This wasn't the distant lightning to which we'd got accustomed; this was not just some feeble flicker of light just above the horizon; these were blue moments of brilliance lighting up the whole yard.

When for the umpteenth time the lightning rendered everything around us visible, I suddenly realized that Strydom's bakkie was no longer parked in its spot. I went back into the house to make sure.

The blanket on the sofa was neatly folded; his drinking glass was no longer on the window sill; his two grey, worn boots that had been kept to one side in the corner were no longer there.

Strydom had gone.

It was his old trick; we were used to it by now and I forgot about it almost immediately.

There was still lots of lightning that night, and now and again light gusts of wind, and once the very distant rumble of thunder. But no rain. And no plane. And not a single word from Mills.

Vusi came to call me the next morning before daybreak. He wanted to show me something in the yard. There was a big strangler fig above the house under which Strydom always parked his bakkie when he stayed over. But he'd been so sick and delirious the night when he arrived that we'd found his bakkie the next morning in the road above the house with the keys still in the ignition and the door wide open. Although the fig tree had long since shed its leaves, I went to park the bakkie in its spot and put the keys away on the pantry shelf; so I knew exactly where the bakkie had been parked for those few days. There was even a large oil stain to confirm this. The oil stain only later attracted our attention. But it was the tracks that Vusi wanted to show me. There was no trace of Strydom's tyre tracks. The whole tract of bare earth under the tree was covered in large baboon tracks as if they'd been patrolling the place all night. Baboons don't easily quit their sleeping quarters in the dark; it takes at least a leopard to flush them out, and even then they'd rather flee to a higher branch or ledge than down to the ground. Strydom must have left somewhere between eleven the previous evening and three in the morning. The baboons could have been there before the time as well, but after his departure they'd trodden the place to dust.

"What do you think, Vusi, what's going on here?"

"*Bayamfuna*." (They're looking for him.)

"Why?"

"*Bafuna ukukhuluma naye.*" (They want to talk to him.)

I didn't interrogate him any further; I could see from his face that he'd already said more than he'd wanted to.

2

When the rain came at long last, it caught us unawares. Possibly because we'd seen it coming but wouldn't believe it. For a few days fleece clouds had drifted past from the north, and that in itself was unusual; we'd gotten used to a dead, grey sky without clouds. Then Mills reported that it was raining in Durban and the airstrip was too wet to use. There were scraps of reports on the radio about thunderstorms in Swaziland and at night now and again you could hear thunder muttering far in the north. But we'd too often before cherished vain hopes.

Three days after Mills's message I went to Mbabala, because there'd been a message that I should phone Professor Stokes. When I emerged from the hills onto the plain, the sky was still its usual morose grey, but there was a small bank of cloud in the middle of nowhere and I could see it was shedding a little shower of rain.

By the time I started descending to the crossings, ten kilometres this side of Mbabala, there was rain behind me. I could see the sky gradually clouding over. The first drops started falling as I crossed the river. Both windows of the bakkie were open and for the first time in three years I got the smell of wet soil again.

By the time I stopped at the station it was raining hard.

Julia and Vukile and Sister Erdmann were trying to herd people into the clinic from outside, but nobody wanted to go in, and those who were in were on their way out. Everyone stood gazing up at the sky, some with their bony arms extended above their heads, some with their mouths wide open to try to taste the drops, some on their knees. One of them, a very tall man I had not seen before, was clapping his hands slowly, and the rest started following his lead one by one. He spoke in a very high-pitched voice. We couldn't understand what he was saying, but some of the others started repeating everything after him. They clapped their hands rhythmically, their cadaverous bodies swaying, and spoke-sang the tall man's praise song after him. We stood among them, all of us, because Sister Roma and Gwaja had in the meantime joined us, and gazed and gazed at the rain. Gwaja started dancing with them. The little bunch of Chopis who were with us in the yard were admittedly the strongest of those remaining at Mbabala, but they were nevertheless all of them just skin and bones and debilitated. In spite of this all of them, big and small, kept time with feet and hips and shoulders to the measure of an inaudible rhythm. I saw Sister Roma starting to dance, and then Vukile, then Julia. Then I joined in the dance. And when she was the only one remaining not dancing, then the weeping Sister Erdmann also danced. We were all of us, each in his own way, I realized, celebrating the Great Process.

3

We went into that autumn with many things around us that we did not even begin to understand. Some of these we couldn't comprehend because we refused to accept them. They were so unreasonable that even a logical explanation, had one been on offer, would not have sufficed for us. Other things again were not so much unreasonable, as just immeasurably unnecessary – or so, at any rate, they seemed to me. And there were yet others that simply passed all understanding.

It started raining early in March, which was unusually late for any summer rainfall region and totally unheard of for a subtropical zone that had had hardly any rain in three years. So, at any rate, meteorologists would have us believe. But when it started raining, it didn't stop again.

On that day of the first shower of rain, I'd arrived at Mbabala in order to phone Stokes. I was sure it would be bad news. He often phoned Julia to pass on this or that message to me. The fact that he wanted to speak to me in person probably spelt the end of the project. I struggled for an hour to get through to him and the line was so noisy that I could hardly hear what he was saying. But he was telling me how important it was for me to stay on "to document the most severe drought in human memory in a very unique region". The "most severe drought" was transformed within three days into what radio reports now called "a terrifying flood disaster".

The little bit that the drought had left us of our "unique region" was being washed away. I was trapped at the mission hospital, because the river was in flood. Every morning and every afternoon we walked down to the crossing, which for a year or more I could ford dry-shod, and we stood watching the brown mass thundering past with its constant yield of booty – tree trunks and the roof poles of huts and kudu cadavers and, once, the body of a child floating along on his back over the waves and washing past near to us.

It rained hard the first night and we celebrated it almost all night. The next day it changed to a fine drizzle that for many days simply persisted. The Chopis had to sleep in the church and the clinic. For the first two days we could still keep cooking fires going outside under the corrugated-iron lean-tos, but from the third day the wood was too wet to start a fire and the two coal stoves in the kitchen had to shoulder the burden alone. We knew that it if it didn't stop raining, the coal would run out within a week.

We phoned de Gaspri to ask if he could deliver a load of coal, but according to the woman who answered the phone, de Gaspri had been trapped by the rain in Mbazwana and the roads to us were in any case totally impassable. Every news bulletin on the radio brought fresh reports of flooding and washed-away bridges and new outbreaks of cholera.

Although Vusi knew how to operate the radio, there was no word from him, nor did he reply when I tried to call him. For three days there was also no reply from Bruyns's Red Cross camp.

On the fourth day an exhausted Bruyns phoned to say that their telephone, like most other phones in Durban, was out of operation, it was still raining there and Jock Mills had for two days been lying catatonically sozzled in a leaking Red Cross tent. For want of a better solution he adopted a philosophical attitude. "There's no point in bringing him round. Every time he wakes up and hears it's still raining, he just starts drinking all over. Seems to me he's sensitive to bad weather."

We lost people every day; sometimes only one, sometimes as many as five a day. The soil was, it was true, soft after all the rain, but it was red clay that clung to the pickaxes and spades in such quantities that digging graves was a battle. The graves, despite our best intentions, became shallower and shallower.

After a week we realized that the rain constituted a greater threat than the drought had ever been. The coal had almost run out and although the sun was starting to shine feebly by day, heavy showers fell every night.

Vukile called us into his office one evening – Julia and me and the two nuns. Gwaja was in the cooking shelters trying to get wet wood to take with paraffin, because it had been drizzling again all afternoon. For a change Vukile was not vague; he came to the point and his message was very simple: "We have to face the facts."

We all knew immediately what he was saying, but Julia was not prepared for the facts just yet and her only defence was to be perverse.

"Tell us about it, Vukile."

"This can go on for a week, a month – who knows? According to this afternoon's count we are a hundred and twelve people. We have enough food here for ten days. What happens then?"

"Bruyns and them can organize a helicopter or something." That was Julia again.

"Just like that? Why didn't we think of that ages ago!"

"Something will happen, Vukile. The weather will clear or something. Mills could…" She remembered about Mills and shut up.

"Is that a wish or a promise?"

"We can't damn well give up hope, Vukile, now can we?"

"We must pray. That's all we can do, brother." That was Sister Roma's sober contribution.

"What do you suggest?" Julia demanded. "We stop feeding these people?"

"We will have to decide about that sooner or later, Julia. And the sooner the better. It's for us to decide whether we are going to sit here and hope for the best or…"

"Or what?"

"Or do something about it!" He was fast losing his temper.

"Do what?"

"Pray. We can pray, Julia." That was Sister Roma again, anxious to restore peace. "God will not disappoint us. He never has."

And that, for Vukile, was the last straw. "You sure? Are you sure about that?" He switched to Zulu. "Where has this God been these last three years?" he demanded. "There are almost a hundred and fifty people buried out there. Where was He when we battled to save their lives? Where was He when night after night we tried to get children of three and four to pull through using reed pipes of porridge water? How many times did you pray then, *mama*? And how many times did it help?"

Sister Erdmann, who was never a great talker, suddenly took a deep breath and got up. How much she'd understood of Vukile's flood of Zulu was anybody's guess, but apparently she'd understood enough.

"If you don't believe in God, brother Vukile, so be it. I know God will save us. Maybe not all of us, but most of us. If you don't want to share your food with these poor people outside, you're welcome. I will not eat again before all of them are safe."

"Neither will I." Sister Roma made a little genuflection and went out.

Julia followed Sister Roma out.

That left only Vukile and me and Sister Erdmann. "I am sorry, brother Khumalo. But we don't have a choice."

"You'll last five or six days – then it's only me left. Then what? Who will feed them then?"

"God will provide." Then she, too, left.

Vukile sat for a long while just staring at the wall. Then he turned to me. "Why didn't you say anything?"

I didn't know what to say to him.

4

In retrospect those few days after the first rains were the only time when Julia and I enjoyed a normal love affair. We ate with Vukile and Sister Roma or Sister Erdmann or Gwaja every evening and then walked back through the drizzling evening rain to her *kaya* and lay on her sagging little cot and, enclosed by the aroma of buchu and incense, listening to the purling of water in the gutters, we spoke about all kinds of things which we'd not had time or courage to touch upon before. And in each other's arms, with the little bit of candlelight around us and the dark rain outside, evening after evening we explored each other's bodies in wonder and with more and more abandon. Time after time I found myself ensnared in her unbelievable mouth and marvelled at the small of her back that fitted the palm of my hand like a violin. Her eyelashes and her fingertips and her breath were the wings of tiny birds on my cheek. We made love and at last, spent and sated and satisfied, drifted into slumber in the snug and secure warmth of each other's body and slept the dead sleep of the innocent.

But after the altercation with Vukile that also started to change. The first evening I assumed she was stressed and tense. Her argument with Vukile was looking for a place to vent itself, and found one when I, alone with her at last, said that I thought Vukile's point of view had merit. "That's to say," I added unwisely, "if I understood correctly what he was trying to say, because it's not exactly as if you and the Sisters gave him a chance to put his case."

"So you also want to sit and eat while they're starving to death."

"That's not what I'm saying. And I'm not at all sure that that's what Vukile was trying to say. But if you don't eat properly, in a week's time you're not going to have the strength to care for the others. And what then?"

It turned into a long, convoluted, senseless argument. All I know is that after a while I realized that we were talking in circles and we were saying things to each other that we could really have done without. I also realized that part of the three women's contrariness was caused by their mostly unexpressed frustration with Vukile Khumalo. Because Vukile had long since become tired of the situation, overworked, sick of struggling. And, unlike them, he had long since stopped really believing in what he was doing. Although that could also be an unjust thing to say, because to the very last I saw him once again, from early to late, sometimes hours after midnight, sitting by dying people, massaging them in an attempt to effect a last little bit of blood circulation.

Julia went to bed and left me in the sitting room.

That night it stopped raining. The next morning was filled with sunlight and sparrows that were starting to explore the eaves for a nesting place. There were midges and spiders on the stoep again and ants scurrying around on the bare yard, starting to build little red ant heaps.

Two days later the river level had dropped enough for me to drive through.

What Vukile did, I don't know, but in those two days Julia and the Sisters did not eat. Nor did I. But not because I was on hunger strike. I just couldn't eat any longer. There were too many people everywhere spewing out the little bits of food that they could get in. Apparently a stomach condition that Vukile couldn't explain was rife. The kitchen was filthy and the rest of the place smelt like a stable. In the succession of rainy days the Chopis had got used to staying indoors. They sat and lay all over the hospital. Even the kitchen was constantly full of people coming to check for leftovers in the cooking pots. Normally Vukile was the one to drive them out when they became a nuisance, but he stopped bothering. They urinated all over the walls. Nobody kept a check any longer. Gwaja was the one who tried to stem the flood with a mop and a pail of water, but the day before I left, five people died and he had to dig another grave.

Vukile assured me it wasn't cholera.

He was tired. I could see he had no strength left in him. You could still from time to time hear his high-pitched little cackle somewhere, but I couldn't help noticing that every time after he'd finished laughing, he took out his handkerchief and wiped the tears from his eyes.

The morning of my departure I woke up just after daybreak. Julia was not in her room. So I walked down to the river to check the water level. It had gone down considerably. I gathered my belongings and loaded them onto the bakkie. Julia was on her way from the church to the clinic in the first bit of sunshine and I walked to meet her.

"Morning, Julia," I said when we were face to face.

"Morning." She said it so softly that I could hardly hear her, and put her arms around my waist and held me tight.

"I'm about to leave, Julia."

Then she looked up at me. "Why?"

"The river has gone down."

I could hear her inhaling very slowly and very deeply and then releasing her breath very slowly.

"I must go and see how things are with Vusi."

"Can I ride along to the river?"

"Yes."

"I just want to make sure you get through."

She got into the front with me and we drove the four hundred metres to the river in silence. I stopped at the edge of the water.

"It still looks very deep to me."

"Half a metre at the deepest."

"Can I walk out in front of you? Just to make sure."

"No, Julia."

"Why not? I'd like to do it."

"You could step into a hole or something."

She got out and kicked off her shoes. "I'll see you on the other side."

"No, Julia. If you fall or something and I stop, I might not get this old thing started again." But she'd walked into the water already.

I waited until she was about ten metres in and then followed. She was walking very slowly and I gradually caught up with her. She'd bundled up her dress in front in an attempt to keep it dry. The deeper the stream became, the more strongly it flowed. Later I could see she was battling. I called at her through the window. "Julia. Listen here." She couldn't or wouldn't hear me. "Get onto the bonnet of the bakkie till the water gets shallower!" I think she couldn't hear me, because the rush of the river was louder than I'd anticipated. "Julia, hang onto the bakkie." She looked round swiftly once as if she wanted to make sure that I was still there and then pushed on again. The water level was dropping and I kept close to her until we reached the other bank.

Her dress was wet up to her navel.

I got out and went to her.

"Thank you."

"Don't mention it."

"Now I'll have to take you back again."

She just laughed. I pulled her closer and held her to me.

"Brand…"

"Yes, never mind. I know."

"What?"

I had no idea what to say to her.

"It won't work out, Brand." There was a moment's hesitation. "No, that's not what I wanted to say."

"What did you want to say?" I held her tighter, because it felt as if she was trying to get away from me.

"I wish I could spend the rest of my life walking ahead of you to make sure that the water's not too deep for you. But I can't, Brand."

"I'll walk ahead of you, Julia."

"You can't."

"Why not?"

"I've wished all my life I could have someone like you. Once I almost thought it was Ulrich, but it turned out not to be. Then I thought it was Jan Tolmay. I know it's you. I've known for sure for the last while that it's you."

"I'm glad, Julia."

"But I can't do it to you."

I pushed her away from me in an attempt to see her face. That's what I'd been expecting her to say, but when she said it, all of a sudden I couldn't believe it.

"Don't look at me, Brand. Hold me a little."

"What is it you can't do to me?"

"I'm not good for you. I'll just complicate things. I'm bad news."

"And what if I loved you? Wouldn't that perhaps make a difference?"

"That just makes it much worse."

I thought she was a bit overwrought. She was tired, after all. She'd been working too hard for too long, slept too little, seen too much. She hadn't eaten for two days. She clearly wasn't thinking straight.

"When all this is over, we may think very differently about many things. I'm coming back in a few days' time. Then we can talk." I held her for a moment. "Come, let me walk with you till you're through the deep end."

"No. Please. You can stand and watch if you like. But I want to walk alone."

"Why?"

"Please."

Then she kissed me swiftly on the mouth and walked into the water.

I stood watching her feeling her way, deeper and deeper, more and more carefully, step by step. When she was in to her middle, she looked round and waved at me. I waited until she'd reached the other side. I hoped she would wave again, but she didn't. She wrung out her skirt and put on her shoes and disappeared among the trees towards the mission station.

That was the last time I saw her.

I heard later that two freight helicopters of the South African Military Medical Services had landed at Mbabala two days later with food supplies. Apparently thanks to Tito de Gaspri who had chanced to say the right thing at the right time to the right person. They took sixty of the Chopis away to a temporary army emergency aid camp at Richards Bay and came to fetch the rest the following day. Julia left with the second load. Apparently she had tried to get hold of me, but my radio was dead. She left a letter that Vukile later gave to me. There was nothing new in the letter. It was just the same things that she'd told me that day by the river. She felt that her work was done at Mbabala. She was on her way to nowhere. She'd let me know when she reached it.

I had for almost a week, every night till late, unsuspectingly sat taking apart the radio again and again and checking it and reassembling it before I spotted the fault and got it going with bits of copper wire and Elastoplast and faith and hope. By the time I could talk to Mbabala again, Julia had been gone for several days.

I'd be violating the truth if I pretended that I found it easy. There are certain things which you violate by trying to talk about them too much. It's been almost five years, and I haven't heard from her again. There was a rumour, once, that she was doing missionary work in Suriname. Perhaps there where she is now she's found a kind of peace that suffices for her. But I still often wake up at night and imagine I hear her opening the door. I know, as you sometimes know such things, that I'll never stop waiting. And God knows it's terrible to think that she may be waiting too.

What is this thing, between one human being and another, that is so vertiginous that it makes the last step towards each other impossible?

5

There were a few light showers after the worst of the rain had cleared, but for the rest of the time the sun was warm. Vusi and I gaped in amazement at the landscape around us that first week. It was March, but the veld was pure spring. The foothills of the Ubombos started shimmering green and in the kloofs the wild plum started sprouting and the wild pear was budding.

But that was after we'd gone looking for Strydom.

The oil stain under the fig tree had bothered me all along. Because Strydom always parked there and there had never been oil before. The fact that we'd found his bakkie on the dirt road and that he'd clearly arrived in some state of delirium that night made me wonder whether he hadn't damaged his sump on the way to us that night. The morning after his mysterious departure Vusi had followed the oil trail for some distance and discovered that Strydom had gone south on the road to Mbabala. Ten days later, when we went looking for the oil trail, it had washed away.

Except in one important spot.

We drove south, very slowly, with Vusi in front on the bonnet looking for signs. In sandy places there was no more oil visible. But on the patches of red soil and on the stone ledges Vusi could still here and there point out faint traces of what a fortnight ago must have been a considerable flow of oil. At that rate of wastage, I knew, Strydom's bakkie wouldn't last long.

The place where he'd turned off was on a flat stone ledge. The oil trail was clear. And it might have seemed like chance, but it was in fact not chance at all. The turn-off had been chosen precisely there, where no one would notice it. I'd driven past there hundreds of times and never seen that there was a turn-off. It was no more than a rocky ledge to the left of the road. The oil trail led us across the ledge to a narrow grass-crested track into the kloofs.

We drove for about three kilometres, through drifts and around piles of rocks and up inclines and through narrow tunnels in the bush into a small clearing. And on the open patch was Strydom's bakkie. Under the canvas canopy there was the usual little pile of books, a bundle of blankets, saucepans, frying pans, a tin mug, a coffee pot, a torn packet of mealie-meal, little hammers, prospector's pans, a toothbrush. No sign of Strydom.

This was where his engine had seized.

We had to hack away branches to get past the bakkie. Five or six kilometres farther the road just petered out in a little bare yard up against a low overhang.

If it hadn't been for the table and chair, you might have thought that you'd reached a dead end. But there was a dilapidated bamboo chair and table under a red ash and, to the left of these, under a large wild orange extending at an angle from under the overhang, was obviously the place where Strydom used to park his bakkie.

The front door was round the corner; a reed curtain in a narrow passage. Behind the curtain it was murky. I struck matches and saw furniture. A table and a chair and a single bed and a cupboard and shelves with books and an oil stove and saucepans. I found a lamp and three candles and lit them and waited for the light to seep into all the dark crannies.

We were in a shallow cave. Three of its sides were rock, one side was a clay-and-lath wall with a small window. Right opposite the window was the reed-curtain entrance. It was a large room, probably easily twenty metres in diameter, the roof invisibly high. With the light gradually gaining the upper hand, one piece of furniture after the other started looming out of the darkness. A large table full of stuff. A high shelf. No, two shelves. Three. Another table. A crate full of tools. A zinc bath. Framed photos on the rock faces. A cardboard box full of magazines. An old gramophone. A wooden box full of twelve-inch records. Box files. Notebooks. A battery radio. Suitcases with clothes. Plastic bags full of cassettes.

The home-made tables and shelves were almost all crowded with pieces of skull and jawbone and pelvic bone and scapula and hand bones. I'm no palaeontologist, but even I could see that there were skulls that I'd never come across in any textbook. Some of them were more or less complete. Others, I gradually saw, had been joined piecemeal with large pieces of plaster of Paris in between to fill in the missing sections.

There was a large table in the centre of the room with a plate and a mug and loose sheets of paper and a few chunks of broken rock. On the table, next to the only chair, next to three quarters of a bottle of muscadel and half a glass of wine, were Strydom's spectacles. The bit of sunlight penetrating the window reflected in the three large cracks in the lenses. It seemed as if the spectacles were doing their utmost to focus on something beyond the window.

That was all we were ever to see of Strydom again.

I drove to his place again a month later, and apart from a few mice scurrying about on the dark floor, everything was exactly the same.

It was only on the second visit that, in the light of a gas lamp I'd brought along, I could take a closer look at the two framed photos on the rock face. One was of a very youthful Strydom next to a thin young girl with unruly curly hair. Strydom is staring straight at the camera, his arm loosely round the girl's waist, and she's laughing and looking out of the photo. Helena. The second photo was a head-and-shoulders of the same girl. This time she was looking straight into the camera lens, and she's laughing again, but this time there's a sadness in that laughing face that haunted me for days.

6

One morning just after daybreak I was woken up by an aircraft flying very low over the house. When I got outside, Vusi was also out in the yard looking up. "What's happening, Vusi?" I demanded. "It sounded as if he wanted to land on the roof."

"*Mfishane*," was all he would say. *Mfishane* ("the short one") was the nickname of the region's people for Mills.

"Are you sure?" It had indeed sounded like the Dakota.

"*Uyaphenduka*." (He's coming back.)

After a while I could hear the droning getting more distinct again. We stood watching the plane coming round the shoulder of the mountain and descending, lower and lower the nearer it came and the next moment tearing right above us – so low that I could see the peeled-off paint under the wing. It was the DC-3.

It turned round again and flew over us and then took wing towards Shabeni.

"He wants to go and fetch petrol. He must be looking for help."

I'd wanted to go to Mbabala that morning, but we crossed the mountain to Shabeni. In places the road was badly washed away and it took more than an hour to get there.

The Dakota was there, at the far end of the runway, the nose turned round already. Jock was carrying drums of fuel up from the cellar.

"Ha!" he said when he saw us. "I hoped you'd come."

"Are you coming to fill up?"

"Yes."

"Are you alone?"

"Yip. Bruyns is too busy; the other guys in the camp are too scared." We started loading the drums onto the bakkie. "Here towards the end I was only too damn glad I didn't have anybody with me. My tanks are bone dry. Things are nice and green around here, aren't they? You should see it from the air. Looks like King's Park. Do you know how much petrol there's left at Mbabala?"

"Almost nothing."

"Guessed as much. If I remember rightly five or so drums. I think we fill both tanks and then I'll load twenty drums or so for the next trip. How many people have you still got there? Will two trips be enough?"

"What people, Jock?"

"Masais. What do you call them? Chopis."

"There are no more Chopis there, Jock."

He was lifting a drum of fuel over the edge of the bakkie. He stopped dead and then carefully placed the drum on the ground.

"What?"

"The army came to fetch them." He just stood staring at me.

"I thought you knew."

"How would I know?" He looked from me to Vusi and back at me, as if he wanted to make sure we weren't making a silly joke. "Did they take them all?"

"So Vukile tells me."

"Oh." He walked around the bakkie and went and stood gazing at the Dakota. "Oh, OK." Then he started walking away from us to the Dakota. Halfway there he stopped dead again and turned back to me. "You're sure?"

"Yes."

"Absolutely?"

"Yes."

There were about five drums of petrol on the bakkie and a few more on the ground. Vusi and I loaded them too and were in the process of carrying another few up from the cellar when we heard the plane's one engine starting up. We clambered up the steps to the top and ran round the bakkie in time to see the second propeller starting to spin. The Dakota's door was closed.

I thought he was testing something. I was imbecile enough to think he was just checking something or other. After all, Mills had said in so many words that both his tanks were empty. I got into the bakkie and started driving towards the airstrip. And saw the Dakota starting to move. Then I stopped and got out and saw the Dakota picking up speed and at last letting go of the earth and climbing into the grey air.

Vusi and I stood next to each other watching Jock Mills's Dakota DC-3 slowly veering north-east, away from Mbabala, and cumbersomely climbing higher and higher and at last disappearing into the great grey void.

There was, as far as I could ascertain, never any mention in the news of a Dakota wreck found in the Mozambique bundu. Who would know? The plane had long since been scrapped from all records. And Mills himself was one of those people that nobody would ever really miss. Everybody who knew him, probably assumed that he'd taken off on his Harley Davidson on a whim in search of pastures new.

The few people that in later years I told about Jock Mills, about Mills and of course about Strydom too, late at night on my little plot of ground, with the evening's wine depleted and the moon a little sliver of light over the mountains, were inclined to sigh and say it was a sad story. I don't think it is. I'm sure Mills planned his death with the same precision as all the other things he'd tackled in his life. His rebuilt DC-3 was his only proof that he could achieve the impossible. And his last moment in that DC-3 was his greatest triumph – far away from the fickle hubbub of applause. And Strydom's story was in a way the same. Perhaps he found what he'd been looking for – a last morsel of bone that fitted exactly between the canine and the seventh molar. He hadn't finished his glass of muscadel. He'd taken off his glasses and placed them on the table. He'd seen enough. That, after all, was that. For him, as for Jock Mills, that in the end was how it was. So.

7

Returning from Shabeni that afternoon I immediately tried to call the mission station by radio. There was more interference on the air than usual and I could only just hear Vukile at the other end.

"Didn't Mills come that way this afternoon?"

"With what? His Harley?"

I told him what had happened but I wasn't sure that he could hear.

Vusi went to his room early that night, because it was full moon. I could hear he was in conference. I sat alone on the front stoep listening to the frogs making the kloof resound in song and counter-song. And in a wash of what Eugène Marais would probably have called Hesperian melancholy I drank to them all. To Vukile because I thought that of all of us he'd probably been given the least credit. He may not have been a brilliant doctor, and he may have been the wrong man in the wrong place, but he had a good heart and for much of the time he did whatever he did in spite of himself. I drank to Jock Mills and to Strydom. To Mills because he'd so badly wanted to be a hero and had been cheated by fate; and in particular I drank to him with feeling because he'd had his last drink. And to Strydom because I didn't know what had happened to him. I lifted my drink to him high up in the darkness and said "So!" and didn't care whether Vusi saw or not, and persuaded myself that total melancholy was perhaps the only condition in which you very vaguely twigged something about your place in the universe.

And I drank to Julia.

8

Nowadays there's a priest again at the mission station. Father Johnny Magagula. We call him Johnny, because his baptismal name is Qhobonyeka. He plays a mean game of poker, but he's a teetotaller. Sister Roma has returned to her ancestors. Gwaja and Sister Erdmann are still there, and a young Cuban doctor who has trouble speaking English. The hospital is considerably bigger and they're building a new church. According to reports, Vukile Khumalo is studying theology at a Bible school of the United Methodist Church at Chicuque in Mozambique.

Sometimes over a weekend I visit Father Johnny. He's living in Julia's *kaya*. The place feels totally different. There is different furniture and different pictures on the walls. The incense has yielded to the smell of old books and tallow candles and pipe tobacco. Sometimes I go to stand on the balcony and listen to her washing dishes behind me in the little kitchen. And often, while waiting for Father Johnny to play a card, I smell the peach and the buchu and the honeysuckle of her body.

We talk a lot while playing poker. We talk about God. Often about God, because about something so totally unknowable there's a lot to say. We talk about love and mortality and heroism and many other enigmas. We talk about the Great Process. He understands much about it, though he's inclined to see it as the Great Invisible Hand. Sometimes Vusi goes along, then we play morabaraba and we talk about people flying away through windows and about will-o'-the-wisp, about blind bats flying in the dark and ancestors coming to us in various shapes. When Qhobonyeka Magagula is present, Vusi talks a bit more readily about all the incomprehensible things he experiences at times. Then I wonder, while listening to him and Johnny talk, what does the sense of direction of fresh-water polyps have to do with God and eternity?

Probably everything.

But I know that there is something alongside these things, or behind all these things, lying hidden in the heart of Africa that nobody has ever managed to touch upon.

I always drive back home on Saturday afternoon. And sometimes, when Vusi is not with me, I turn off and drive to the Bápe and climb up the opposite rock face and wait for the troop.

Malume always comes to sit right in front of me. Across the precipice; five metres from me. Then we sit looking at each other. He with his head half thrown back, his eyes piercing as if wishing away the dusk that will bring with it the great and nameless grief.

We don't move. We watch the light stealing away from the kloofs and making its way over the mountains. We sit waiting for darkness.

At first I'd always thought that in that last little bit of light he was looking at me as if expecting something from me, wanting to know something to which only I had the answer.

Now I'm no longer so sure.